The One That Got Away Twice

BY A NEW WRITER

Divyasreemagesh

A Teenage Love Story

First Edition – 2025
ISBN: [978-93-344-0717-4]
Cover Design: Divyasree M
Published by Divyasree M

Dedication

For the ones who found laughter in loneliness and courage in silence, and to all the pure-hearted people who know only to be transparent like a mirror and love deeply without limits—especially the givers.

Acknowledgements

I want to thank everyone who believed in me when I doubted myself, my friends who encouraged this story, and the quiet moments that became words on these pages.

CHAPTERS

PROLOGUE

The first time she left home, she thought she was escaping a cage. But she never imagined freedom would come with loneliness, awkward silences, and moments that make your heart feel too big for your chest.

There was a girl—fond of nothing but loving. She didn't have big dreams, just a simple one: to make her parents proud. Always the giver, never the taker. Innocent. Unaware of how cruel the world can be. Her name was Thinovika. An idiot, if you asked her—interested in everything, but never for too long.. Anyway, this is not a boring story. Because when fate writes your script without asking, even an idiot can end up with a tale worth telling.

The Beginning

chapter 1
The Beginning

Thino went to college with her Dad. Both of them tired from the journey. Excited? Maybe him. Nervous? Definitely her. It was St.Joseph's College of Engineering and Technology—her first sight of it. The building stood tall, and for a moment, she was in awe. "So this is what a college looks like..." I thought. They arrived way too early—6 AM sharp. Typical Asian parent energy. Her registration was only in the afternoon, but her Dad wanted to be ready for war. While they sat near the main block, she noticed something strange. Students. Walking into classes. With books. Studying. Even at that ungodly hour. "Wait, what? Everyone here studies like this? Like... without wasting a second?" she whispered a silent prayer. "Ganapathi, save me for god's sake Please." Her Dad turned to her, smiling. "See how hard they study, Thango? Must be a good college. You study well too." she just stared at him. "Ahh this man..." After registration, they returned to their hometown.

The next few days blurred together in a haze of shopping, packing, and awkward family conversations. New clothes, hostel essentials, and snacks tucked carefully into bags—every little item carried the weight of departure. The emotions in the house ran so deep that silence often felt safer than tears.

Then came a call from her brother. His teasing voice spilled through the receiver, light and mischievous. "Oii! Heard you got into college at Karaikudi—the land of non-veg heaven! Lucky girl, huh? From now on, it's gonna be only eating, sleeping, and chilling!" She laughed softly, though a nervous edge lingered in her tone. "You think so? Then the opposite is definitely going to happen."

"Don't jinx it," he warned in mock seriousness. "You better not prove me wrong!"

"Thanks for the optimism. Now get lost." The line went dead, but a smile lingered on her lips. That silly exchange, ordinary as it was, made everything feel suddenly and terrifyingly real.

Later, the sharpness of her mother's voice echoed from the kitchen, filled with frustration and hurt. "Hey! Are you even listening? Going that far away just for college—this is too much! You people make decisions like I don't even exist. Fine, do whatever you want. I won't interfere anymore!"

Her words pierced the girl's heart, yet when she finally spoke, her voice was soft, almost trembling: "Mommy... I just want a break. I want to go. I need to go. I've had enough of this place... of everything." Her mother fell silent, muttering only, "Fine. Do what you want." The words were low, but the storm within her had not passed; it lingered, quiet yet fierce. That night, the girl lay on her bed, staring at the ceiling as if it might hold the answers she longed for. Every corner of the room pressed its memories against her, making it feel like a final farewell.

A thought echoed in her chest—heavy, yet strangely liberating: after this, she would finally be free. No more arguments, no more rules, just herself, learning to shape her own life. And then, far too soon, the morning of her departure arrived.

They left together—mother, father, and daughter—dragging not only their bags but also the weight of heavier hearts. After hours of travel, the college gates came into view once more, and under the sun that seemed to melt away her confidence, the girl felt smaller with every step. An orientation program awaited, a gathering of parents and students, but while her body was present, her mind wandered elsewhere, quietly counting how many faces she would have to avoid meeting. She had no desire to talk, not out of arrogance, but because somewhere along the way she had forgotten how to trust.

The hostel was chaos—parents rushing, students hauling bags, corridors blocked as if the building itself were too small to hold so many dreams and fears at once. To her, it felt less like a college hostel and more like a crowded theatre just before a grand performance. At last, she and her mother reached Room No. 9. Inside, two girls were already settled, laughing and talking with the ease of childhood friends, their energy clicking together as though they had known each other forever. She lingered in the doorway, smiling politely, nodding here and there, all the while hoping she didn't look too lost. A few questions escaped her lips—small, safe ones—before she slipped away to the restroom to freshen up.

Cold water splashed against her face, and as she met her own eyes in the mirror, she whispered softly, "You can do this, Thino. You can talk to them. Be normal. Make friends." It sounded simple enough, yet simplicity vanished when the past was littered with betrayals, when even smiles had carried conditions. Trust was not something she carried lightly. Returning to the room, she asked the girls if they might bring her some water on their way out. Their kind smiles met her hesitation with warmth. "No problem!" they said. She thanked them, and for the first time that day, hope stirred quietly within her—maybe, just maybe, this was a good sign.

That night, she and her mother shared the narrow hostel bed, neither finding much sleep. Perhaps it was because they both knew this would be the last time they lay side by side like that—just the two of them—for a long while. Her mother held her close, her voice low and trembling as she whispered, "Don't trust people so easily, Thino. This world is harsh. Do your own work. Don't depend on anyone like you did today."

She turned to her mother, confusion clouding her face. "What did I even do?" she asked. "You asked them to fetch water, didn't you?" came the reply. "That's just... a small thing." But her mother only sighed. "You did it because you would have done the same for them. But they're not you. I overheard one of them say, 'There's always that one girl who acts too nice. It's kind of irritating.'" And just like that, her trust cracked again. She didn't argue. She only turned away and muttered, "Fine, Mom," though inside something quietly folded in on itself.

The next morning passed quickly. She had breakfast with her parents in a nearby hotel, but the food was disappointing, leaving the table heavy with silence. Her brother's playful teasing rang in her memory—From now on, only eating, sleeping, and fun ahh, Thinovika? She almost smiled. Like that idiot said... guess I can't escape. Soon after, goodbyes were exchanged. No dramatic tears, no movie-scene hugs—just a quiet, heavy parting. Her lips curved into a smile, but inside her heart shrank, tight and aching.

That evening, after her first class, she returned to the hostel. Everything felt... fine. Not wonderful, not unbearable, just fine. She ate dinner alone, her plate balanced before her as the hall buzzed with chatter. Her roommates had already finished and were laughing with others as though they had known them forever. She told herself it didn't matter. But it did. Sitting down, she took her first bite, and the silence pressed in—not the noise around her, but the silence within. She missed home. She missed being understood without needing to explain herself. And for the first time since arriving, the tears came uninvited.

Her phone buzzed suddenly—a conference call from her family. Mom. Dad. Brother. Sister. She wiped her face quickly, drew in a shaky breath, and forced herself to sound casual as she answered. "Is everything okay, ma?" her mother asked gently.

That single sentence broke down the fragile wall she had built. Tears spilled freely—silent at first, then unstoppable. She cried and cried, minutes stretching into what felt like hours, while her family stayed on the line, each voice taking turns to soothe her. They reminded her she was stronger than she thought, that things would get better, that she wasn't truly alone—even when it felt that way. And for the first time that day, she let herself believe them. Just a little.

The Cursed Room And The Meme Page

chapter 2
The cursed room and the meme page

That night, after dinner, she wandered alone near the mess block, the hostel lights flickering above her like something out of a low-budget horror film. That was when she noticed it—a door left slightly ajar. The room beyond was dark, dusty, and unsettlingly still. Curiosity tugged at her, and before she could stop herself, she pushed it open. Inside stood old wooden shelves, broken furniture scattered carelessly, and cobwebs that seemed older than her. The silence pressed in so heavily that her mind supplied its own soundtrack—something straight out of The Conjuring. She turned slowly, her heart thudding... and there it was. A face. Right behind her. She jumped so violently she nearly dropped her phone. But it wasn't a ghost. It was just a girl—round baby face, chubby cheeks, and long straight hair, like a porcelain doll with a slightly eerie charm. The stranger looked at her calmly, as if she belonged there all along.

"By the way... where's Room No. 9?" a girl asked suddenly, catching her off guard. Still drained from the long day, she blinked before answering, "Nine? That's my room. Why?" The girl smiled, almost shyly. "Oh, I think I'm your roommate." Of course she was. They walked back together, and along the way another girl joined them—Kavya. She was sharp-eyed and quick-tongued, the kind of person who seemed to notice everything. "So, which batch are you from?" she asked, tilting her head with curiosity. "Uh... 2020," came the hesitant reply.

Kavya's eyebrows shot up in mock surprise. "Ohh... you're my senior then. You look young. I'll call you akka!" Me? Akka? She half-laughed, half-cringed, uncertain if she liked the sudden promotion to "big sister." And just like that, the ghost-room found its life, with a surprise roommate, a lively new companion, and a brand-new title for her in a place where she still didn't even know where the bathrooms were.

A few days slipped by, and her roommate began blending easily with the other two girls, their voices rising together in bursts of laughter that spilled into the corridors like music. But she herself did not melt into that circle so easily. She lingered at the edges, smiling faintly, pretending it didn't matter. She told herself it wasn't jealousy, that she was fine on her own—but in truth, disappointment pressed quietly at her chest, heavier than she wanted to admit.

They watched movies together, shared snacks, and laughed at inside jokes that seemed to bloom overnight, the kind that didn't need any explaining. They invited her too, kindly, more than once—but each time she turned them down. Adapting wasn't that easy for her. So while they huddled around the same screen, shoulders touching in easy friendship, she curled up with her laptop, disappearing into the familiar comfort of K-dramas. Everything was fine, she told herself... just not quite the way she had imagined it would be.

A week slipped by in a rhythm of new routines. She and her friend Kavya often walked to college together, sharing small conversations that made the unfamiliar campus feel a little less intimidating. One day, during the induction program, a tall boy stepped onto the stage. He carried himself with an ease that drew every eye—charming, confident, and bursting with energy. Every college had that guy, the one everyone seemed to orbit around. For them, it was Ravi—the Club Hero.

He took the mic, his voice booming across the hall, "Welcome to the jungle, juniors! Clubs here don't just make events—we make memories. Come join the madness!" The crowd erupted in cheers, girls swooned, phones lifted, and cameras flashed. She sat back quietly, watching the spectacle. Amused? Yes. Impressed? Not at all. When Ravi sang a song, the auditorium nearly shook with excitement. His voice was good, she admitted, but there was something in her that resisted the charm. If everyone loved someone, she usually didn't care much. That was just who she was. Still, she couldn't deny it—he did sing well.

Later that night, scrolling aimlessly through Instagram, an idea struck her like lightning. With a grin, she created a meme page under the name "trouble_double" and posted a cheeky meme about Ravi. It blew up instantly. By the next morning, the whole college was buzzing with whispers and notifications—Who's running this page? The mystery only fueled the excitement. Post after post followed, filled with memes about campus life, students' feelings, and inside jokes only the college crowd would understand. The page caught fire, spreading faster than she had ever imagined.

A week later, their class finally got its official classroom, and as expected, she headed straight for the last bench. A girl was already sitting there—thin, with long straight hair, and a face that faintly resembled the actor Manobala.

When she turned suddenly, almost with a startled brightness, they exchanged a silent glance that seemed to ask, What now? Gathering her courage, she asked, "Can we sit here?" The girl hesitated, then replied, "Hmm... okay. Another girl said she'll come, but fine—you can." Soon, the lecturer walked in and the class began. About an hour later, a tall girl with curly hair and Gandhi-style glasses entered, late. Her voice was bold, deep, and filled with confidence as she asked, "Sirr... may I come in?" Heads turned—including hers. The girl walked up to their bench and looked at the straight-haired one. "Where's my spot?" she asked, only to be told, "They came before you... what to do. Go there, there's space." With a shrug, the curly-haired girl went and sat beside their bench.

When the class ended, introductions finally began. Kavya asked for their names. The straight-haired girl replied, "Harini," while the one with the curly hair said, "Yazhini." Then Yazhini looked at her and asked with sudden recognition, "Wait, are you the girl from Dharmapuri?" Surprised, she nodded. "Yeah... how do you know that?" Yazhini grinned. "Of course I know! I'm from the same wing, next to your room.

I've come by a few times. I know your roommates too. Our rooms are close." Embarrassed, she admitted, "Ohhh, really? Sorry... I don't really pay attention to people. I was probably lost in a K-drama or something." Yazhini's eyes lit up instantly. "Wait, wait—you watch K-dramas? I do too!" She blinked, startled, before smiling. "Really?? Which one's your favorite?" At the same time, both of them said, "Goblin." They burst out laughing, the awkwardness dissolving in an instant. As they continued chatting, a notification popped up on her phone, and Harini caught a glimpse of her lock screen. "You're a Thalapathy fan??" she exclaimed. She grinned proudly. "Yeah, of course!" And just like that, a bond was born.

For reasons she couldn't quite explain, a strange sense of comfort settled around her, and because of them, she slowly began opening up to others as well. Week by week, the three of them grew closer, becoming a gang of their own.

Every weekend was filled with karaoke, dancing, and laughter that made the hostel walls echo with joy. They were golden days, shimmering and carefree. Yet somewhere in those weeks, she felt herself changing—like she was slowly turning into someone new, someone she hadn't met before.

The Innocent Man And Her Changes

chapter 3
The Innocent Man and her Changes

On New Year's night, while the hostel buzzed with girls buried in assignments, she too sat scribbling away, lost in deadlines. Suddenly, a girl rushed into her room, breathless with excitement, shouting, "Ravi's live on Instagram! Come watch!" She joined in with the others, their eyes glued to the screen where Ravi and his friends filled the frame—performing, laughing, entertaining an unseen audience from some hotel stage. But as she watched, her attention slipped past the music, past the charm, and landed elsewhere. In the background, almost unnoticed, stood a boy. Not the star, not the noise—just him.

The camera shifted slightly, catching his face for a fleeting moment. He wasn't singing, wasn't trying to shine. He was simply there, quiet and steady, with eyes that carried a softness, a calm she hadn't seen before. And just like that, he had her attention.

The next day, while editing clips from that live, she lingered longer than usual on the frames where he appeared. A friend passing by peeked at her screen and chuckled, "Hey... you even added the club Chairman too!" She froze, blinking. "Uhh... what club Chairman?" The friend laughed harder. "You didn't know? That's him! You're editing this without even knowing who he is?" The realization stunned her. All this time—so polite, so silent, always in the background—and he was the club Chairman? She felt foolish for not knowing.

Still, she finished the edit and posted it on the meme page. Soon, club members were sharing it, tagging each other, laughing in the comments. To her shock, even the club Chairman himself shared it to his story. That tiny gesture filled her with an unexpected happiness that lingered through the evening.

But that night, the high came crashing down. Her enemy arrived—periods and mood swings, raw and merciless. She had been so caught up in editing, so lost in the rush of it all, that she had completely forgotten about the series test the next day. The syllabus felt endless, the words on the pages blurred, and no matter how hard she tried, nothing would stick. Overwhelmed, she broke down and cried—without reason, without restraint. Kavya sat beside her patiently, offering siddha medicine for the cramps, whispering comfort until the pain dulled and the tears slowed. She eventually fell asleep, the books still unopened. Somehow, the next morning, she managed to face the exam. And that was life—chaotic, exhausting, and yet, in its own way, beautifully messy.

And day by day, she changed. Not in a dramatic, slow-motion, movie-montage kind of way, but quietly, naturally, like a flower blooming in the background of someone else's story. She started laughing more, started talking more, started trusting more. She became someone she had never been before—almost an extrovert. Well, a functional one. Kavya, Harini, and Yazhini somehow made her feel like she belonged, and it was bizarre.

The same girl who once couldn't hold a conversation without second-guessing every word now cracked jokes in the corridor like she owned the place. She went on trips—yes, her, the "cry-alone-in-a-corner" type.

She even went to a temple. A temple, can you believe it? All because of that curly-haired menace—Yazhini. It was one of those spontaneous Sunday plans. Harini barged in with her usual chaos and declared, "Get ready. We're going to the temple." She blinked. "I'm what now?" Harini didn't even let her argue. "You're coming. No arguments. Wear something decent." She should've said no, really should've, but she didn't. And so she found herself standing in front of some ancient gopuram, questioning every life decision that had led her to wake up early on a weekend.

But then they sat under a shady tree near the temple, laughing over cheap sundal and bad jokes. Preetha was mimicking one of their lecturers, Kavya was recording everything for "evidence," and Harini kept feeding her prasadam like she hadn't eaten in years. And in that moment, she realised she wasn't bored—not even a little. Somehow, these idiots had turned even a temple trip into a memory. And just like that, the gang was official.

No group name. No secret handshake. Just shared lunches, mutual sarcasm, and emotional breakdowns scheduled between 10 PM and midnight.

They didn't choose each other, but they stayed. And in college, that's rarer than love. That's how the gang formed—not with a bang, but with endless conversations that never needed a reason to begin.

Two Mafias

chapter 4
Two Mafias

It started with a whisper. Well, technically—with a horror face and overacting. But let's just call it... dramatic delivery. Kavya and I had become thick as thieves by then. Closer than hot dosas and coconut chutney. We shared everything—snacks, gossip, even eye-rolls during boring lectures. So naturally, I couldn't keep the secret from her any longer. She had to know. I walked up to her one day, slow and deadly serious, like a villain in a bad soap opera. Eyes wide. Expression tight.

"Kavya..." I said in a low voice. She turned around, startled. "Hey... y-yeah? What's wrong with you? Why do you look like a possessed cat?" I didn't blink. Didn't smile. With a tiny smirk crawling onto my face, I said, "I have something to say." Her eyebrows shot up. "Something? What something?" I leaned in closer. "Do you know the meme page that's been trending in our college?" Kavya blinked. "Of course I do! How can I not know that? It's been spamming my timeline all week. People are going crazy trying to figure out who's behind it. Even some guys made a guessing list. But why are you bringing this up?" I straightened my back.

"Actually..." "Actually?" "Actuallyyyyyyyyy..." "ACTUALLYYYYY?" By then she was two seconds away from throwing her slipper at me. And she did worse—she smacked me right on the head. "Aaaa!" I yelped. "Just say it, you idiot!" she scolded. I rubbed my head and mumbled, "That's actually... me." She froze. Blink. Blink. "You?" she whispered. "You... what??" "I'm the admin," I said, almost proud. "You?" Her eyes widened, like I'd just said I was Vijay's secret twin sister. "You?? The dumb girl who panics during viva and forgets her lunch box?" She blinked again.

"You're running that meme page??" "Dumb? Me??" I folded my arms. Kavya squinted, suspicious. "You're joking. Stop pranking me. You found out I like the page and now you're messing with me." "I'm not joking." "For real?" Her mouth dropped open. Then she did the unthinkable—she shouted. "YOU'RE THE ADMIN, THINOOOOOO!???" I smacked her on the head this time. "Ushhhhhh! Keep your voice down! Are you trying to get us arrested?" "Okay, okay..." she whispered dramatically. Then grabbed my arm and shouted again: "IS THE ADMIN REALLY YOU???" "IDIOT!" I whisper-yelled, looking around.

"You've got no volume control! You'll get me caught!" Kavya, still half-shocked, looked at me like she'd just discovered water on Mars. "How can a mud like you create those memes? Are you actually that... expressive?" I laughed. "No no... I just started because I was bored. But after a few posts, the page blew up. It kind of became... addictive." She looked at me for a second. And then her expression changed. She smiled wide. "Dude. You've got talent." There was pride in her voice. Like she'd discovered a hidden weapon in her team. I smiled back. Maybe for the first time, I believed it a little. From that day on, it wasn't just me. It was us. Kavya joined the madness. We brainstormed meme ideas, pulled all-nighters editing reels, created secret folders full of screenshots, jokes, and club gossip. We didn't sleep. We posted. And slowly, the entire campus buzzed louder than ever before. The meme page wasn't just trending anymore—it ruled. And people still didn't know who was behind it. They only called us one thing: The Criminal Duo. The Meme Mafias. And trust me... The chaos was just getting started.

It was one of those random hostel nights—Thinovika and Kavya lazing around in the so-called "ghost room," the dim light barely filling the corners, their legs stretched on the bed, a phone in hand, and a freshly posted meme glowing on the screen. They were just killing time when suddenly a notification pinged. Kavya snatched the phone before Thino could, glanced at the name, and her eyes widened in shock.

"The Chairman... the club Chairman messaged you?!" she gasped, practically shaking the phone. "The same man who acts like he isn't even interested in anything? He texted you? Girl, we are something!"
Thino leaned over, pretending to be calm, and snatched the phone back. With a smirk tugging at her lips, she read his message. It was short, almost teasing: I'll find you soon. No matter what. She grinned to herself, thumbs dancing across the screen as she replied, Oh really? Then give it a try.
Days passed before she felt cheeky enough to text him again. Looks like you've found out who I am? she teased. His reply came swiftly: You're the girl from my club, aren't you? She laughed, tossing in a playful emoji before answering, That girl from IT? Yeah, I know her too. But Vishwa's reply struck differently: Of course I know her. Because I'm talking to her right now... don't you know that?

Thino froze, smirk still lingering as her mind raced. Was he bluffing, or had he really figured it out? She typed carefully, So you're confirming I'm that girl from your club... I thought you'd never find me. But damn, you almost did. His response was both sharp and patient, like a quiet promise: I'll find you. Sooner or later. Even if you vanish behind memes—a thief who steals for many days will one day be caught. She chuckled, tossing the phone aside for a moment before writing back, Great spirit! Let's see how far you can go, Mr. Sherlock.

And then came the day she hadn't expected. For the first time, Vishwa came to their department. Thino stood in the corner, pretending not to care, but her eyes betrayed her as they followed him. Up close, he wasn't jaw-dropping handsome, nor did he try to be. But something about his presence—the calmness in his eyes, the quiet confidence he carried—pulled her in deeper than she wanted to admit.

He walked in with his crew—Ashwin and the others—though all eyes immediately landed on Ashwin, loud and charismatic, grinning at everyone like he owned the room.

"Excuse me, sir..." Ashwin called out as they stepped inside.

A few minutes later, they entered the classroom with an ease that only seniors could pull off.

"Hey guys! Sooo... do you know who we are?" Ashwin asked, already knowing the answer.

"Talent crew!" the class chorused with excitement.

"Nice! So here's the deal—we're conducting an absolutely FUN event this weekend. Games, memes, madness! And none of you are allowed to skip."

"WE WON'T!" the juniors shouted back.

All the while, Vishwa remained mostly silent, standing a little behind, smiling softly, observing more than speaking. And that smile—gentle, quiet, almost reserved—stirred something in Thino she couldn't quite explain.

As the boys were about to leave, the class burst into goodbyes. "Bye Ashwin! Bye senior! Byeee!" Ashwin waved like a celebrity, soaking in the attention. But then, without meaning to, Thino's voice slipped out. A soft, unplanned, "Hi Vishwa..."

He heard it. He turned.

Her heart leapt into her throat as she clapped a hand over her mouth and ducked behind a chair, cheeks burning, pulse racing. Did I just say that out loud? she thought frantically.
Vishwa, on the other hand, frowned slightly as he walked out, muttering to Ashwin, "Why are these first years giving us so much attention lately?"
Ashwin only laughed, tossing a careless reply. "There's a person behind it."
But Thino remained hidden, heart pounding, face flushed, a silly smile playing on her lips. Because for reasons she couldn't quite name, that quiet boy had already stolen a corner of her thoughts.

The Blast Program

chapter 5
The Blast Program

A few days later, the much-hyped weekend blast finally arrived. We didn't treat it like some big deal, just me, Kavya, and our usual gang of four walking into the hall mostly out of curiosity. Kavya pulled me by the wrist, teasing, "Come on, Thino... it's not a courtroom. Loosen your face." I laughed and told her, "I am loose... I'm just here for the vibe, okay?" But honestly, the real reason I went was to see him. That calm, mysterious, unreadable guy—Vishwa.

The moment we stepped in, it felt like entering a dream. Too many lights, too much sound, too many people. A thousand conversations all overlapping, all happening at once. Sara looked around and muttered, "Bro, this looks like a marriage hall that turned into a DJ zone." Ananya smirked, "If marriage halls had talent like this, I'd actually attend one." And right there in the middle of it all was Ashwin—the star, the showman. He held the mic like it belonged to him and shouted, "EVERYBODY READY?!" The crowd erupted with a wild "YEEESSSSSSSSS!!" Lights burst, confetti flew, and the crowd exploded as the music began.

They kicked off with a fast-paced, high-energy group performance. Ashwin's voice was thunder, his movements magnetic, confident, larger than life. Kavya nudged me with a grin. "Okay okay, Mr. Starboy has entered the chat." I smiled, but my eyes were searching beyond him. And then, he walked in. No spotlight.

No hype. Just stepped onto the stage like it was any other day—Vishwa. He wasn't trying to impress. No wide grin, no loud shout. Just calm. As calm as the moon under the brightest lights, yet somehow brighter than all of them. My breath caught.

"Oh god... why is he like this..." I whispered under my breath as he began singing. His voice wasn't loud or showy—it was smooth, deep, and controlled. And it hit me. Like a thousand petals blooming at once inside my chest. "Why does this feel like a movie...?" I whispered to Kavya, unable to look away. She replied softly, "Because you're the main character, da." I laughed lightly, but my heart was racing like a fire alarm. I couldn't blink. Couldn't move. I just stood there, completely still, watching him. Listening. And in that moment, something inside me shifted.

The crowd clapped, recorded, cheered, but I just kept staring. For the first time, I didn't see him as the club Chairman, or as a senior. I saw him as Vishwa.

That calm voice. That effortless presence. It was overwhelming, not because he tried to be charming, but because he didn't even try. My mind raced: What is this feeling...? I don't even like guys like him. So why now?
When the performance ended, the crowd screamed, phones went up, confetti showered again, and everyone stood up. Ashwin yelled, "THANK YOU, GUYS!! We'll see you next weekend—same time, same madness!"

Vishwa, quieter, added with a light smile, "Take care... and don't forget to register." As the boys walked offstage, the crowd shouted: "Bye Ashwin!" "Bye seniors!" "Bye Vishwai!" And then, out of nowhere, someone yelled—"HI HARI!!"

He paused, turned for a moment. My heart stopped. My hand flew to cover my mouth, eyes wide. "Did I just say that out loud?!" I muttered in panic, ducking behind a chair. Kavya stared at me, speechless. Vishwa, walking away with the group, frowned slightly, wondering, Did I... just hear someone call me? Ashwin laughed and clapped him on the back. "Why are we getting this much attention from first years suddenly..." Vishwa asked quietly. Ashwin grinned, "Maybe you're finally becoming popular, da."

The blast weekend ended, but something from it lingered—the memory of that moment. The moment her heart decided to jump off a cliff, all because of him. Monday came, dragging along the usual college routine, and by afternoon it was time for their library class. Supposedly a quiet hour, but with her group, quiet was never in the plan. As always, the four of them walked in together, each carrying their own version of mischief.

Yazhini did what she always did—scanned the library like it was her personal Tinder. She nudged Thino and whispered, "Oiii look at that junior... new face, fresh face... should I or should I not?" Thino smirked and shot back, "Girl, this is a library, not a lineup."

Meanwhile, Harini had already vanished somewhere near the kids' section, flipping through pop-up books with the excitement of a lost kindergarten teacher. “This book has a pandaaa... look, Kavyaaa!” she yelled from across the shelves. Kavya sighed, shaking her head. “She's gone again.” Thino, on the other hand, drifted between pretending to search for a novel and secretly hoping not to run into anyone from that weekend. They weren't studying.

They were laughing, whisper-yelling, walking around like they owned the shelves. The class ended, but their bickering followed them out through the glass door that separated the library from the corridor. And that's when it happened.

A boy came running from the other side and collided straight into Thino. Her bag slipped, spilling pens, crumpled papers, and even a lip balm that rolled dramatically like a movie scene. Embarrassed, she dropped to her knees, scrambling to gather everything. “Sorry! Sorry sorry sorry—I didn't—sorry!!” she stammered. And then she looked up. Him. Vishwa. That same calm aura. That same unreadable expression. But now, only a few feet away.“I'm sorry, maa... I didn't see you,” he said, his voice soft and sincere. Thino's mind screamed, Not again. Not again. NOT AGAIN. Her heart took off like it was preparing for a relay race. “It's okay... no worries...” she muttered, grabbing the last paper before bolting out the door, past the shelves, not daring to look back. Behind her, Kavya had witnessed the entire thing. She didn't say a word. Just gave her that knowing, teasing smile.

Outside the library, Thino stopped near the stairs, clutching her knees, trying to catch her breath. "Oh my god... I forgot to breathe..." she whispered, taking a long inhale. But her heartbeat refused to slow. Yazhini arrived first, frowning. "Dai, what's wrong with you?" she asked. Kavya, still grinning, dropped the truth like a spark. "Actually... she likes him."

Harini gasped, eyes wide. "Whaaatttt?? THIS idiot likes someone?! WHO?" Kavya, calm as ever, replied, "That guy. The one she just crashed into." Yazhini squinted. "Him??" Harini's jaw dropped. "THAT GUY?? Reallyyyyyyy?? Thinoooooooo!" she shrieked, pointing dramatically. Yazhini playfully smacked Thino on the head. "Stop acting like you're shy now."

Thino panicked, waving her hands. "No no noooo! That's not true! It's not like that!" Kavya tilted her head, teasing, "Mmm... maybe she likes himmm... I think sooo..." Harini exploded. "MAYBE?! I THINK?! YOU IDIOT! Don't say it like it's nothing!" Yazhini crossed her arms. "So you don't like him?"

"YES, YES– I mean NO! Of course not! What even? No change in this lifetime!" Thino stammered, her laugh awkward and unconvincing. The three of them stared at her, unimpressed by the world's worst denial. Kavya chuckled quietly, her smile mischievous. "This is gonna be interesting..."

Crush Promotion

chapter 6
Crush Promotion

It started happening slowly. From time to time, Thinovika would spot him. Not planned. Not expected. But always enough to make her stomach flutter like a paper kite. In the crew block, he would pass by while organizing something. In the department, she would see him casually talking to a senior. At the canteen, he would be standing quietly in a corner, sipping juice while the others shouted over parotta. Even in the library, he sat flipping through pages like time didn't exist. He never said a word, never seemed to notice her, maybe. But she admired him from afar—not in a cheesy "he's so dreamy" kind of way, but because his silence had a weight to it. A peace. A calm she hadn't known in people before.

One random afternoon in class, Thinovika sat at her usual last bench spot, eyes drifting toward the window, her mind nowhere close to the board. Lost in thoughts. Lost in him. Suddenly, a hand snapped in front of her face. Kavya was grinning. "It turns out finally..." she teased. Thinovika blinked. "Turns what?" Kavya leaned in with a knowing look. "You're gone, da. Fully gone." Thinovika frowned in confusion.

"Gone where...?" Kavya chuckled, raising her eyebrow. "Into la-la land. Say it out loud... You have a crush, right?" Thinovika turned her head slowly, lips pressed tight, trying not to show too much, but the smile betrayed her. It broke through anyway. "Crush? Hmm... do you think so?" she whispered. Kavya smacked her arm playfully. "Do I think so? It's written all over your dumb face, Thino! You smile like a K-drama heroine whenever you spot him." Thinovika hid her face with a textbook, muffling a laugh. "Hmmm... maybe yesss..." Kavya only smirked with a proud smile. "I thought it right," she said, and they both laughed quietly, careful not to alert the teacher. But inside Thinovika, something bloomed—a feeling she hadn't allowed herself to admit until now.

Yes. A crush. Not the dramatic, heart-racing, fantasy-type, but the soft kind. The peaceful kind. The kind that grows slowly like a secret between the heartbeat and the smile. And maybe—just maybe—this was the beginning of something she didn't see coming.

The next weekend came around. Another post. Another meme uploaded on her page. The usual chaos in comments followed—fire emojis, "relatable da" comments, and dozens of tags. And then, his name appeared. This time, he texted. A notification popped up on Instagram. Vishwa's DM read: "Repeating that again... A thief who steals for many days will one day be caught. Ma." Thinovika froze. That ma. That playful-yet-suspicious tone. The nerve. But God, her heart did a somersault. Not to be dramatic, but chills spread across her arms. She giggled before replying: "It looks like that... Let's see how the fate turns, hmm?"

There was a pause. He saw the message. Typing... stopped. Typing again... and then: “Hmmm...” Just that. Three letters. But it hit differently. Like he knew. Like he had almost figured it out. Like this game they were playing was slowly becoming real. Thinovika just stared at the screen, smiling, blushing like an idiot, while her heart whispered: “Does he really know it’s me?” Or worse, “Does he know and still text anyway?” She didn’t care. She didn’t want the game to end yet. Let him guess. Let her pretend. The mystery was getting addictive.

That sleepy afternoon unfolded like any other, with Thinovika and Kavya dragging themselves back to class after lunch, yawning between half-hearted jokes. Neither of them hurried; they were simply existing, shuffling their way down the corridor. Kavya rambled on, her voice playful as always, “So... Vishwa’s still going all Sherlock. He’s actually serious about finding the meme admin, you know that?” Thinovika barely reacted, nodding absently while scrolling through her phone. But then her screen lit up, a soft buzz in her palm. She glanced down casually—only to freeze. Her legs stopped moving, her mind emptied, and even the simple act of breathing slipped her memory. Kavya, walking ahead and still mid-sentence, turned back and frowned. “Oiiii... Thino? Did you die or what? I just said his name, why so dramatic?” Thinovika didn’t answer. She stood like a statue, phone clutched in trembling hands, eyes wide. Kavya’s own eyes narrowed suspiciously until it clicked. “Wait... no, no, no, nooo... OH. MY. GOD. This is not good. Don’t die on me, woman!”

Thinovika finally moved, but only to slowly raise the phone toward her friend like a zombie offering proof of life. Kavya leaned closer, glanced at the screen, and froze too.

Her voice dropped to a stunned whisper. "Whaaaatttttt—?!" And just like that, both of them turned into mannequins, planted firmly in the middle of the classroom doorway. A passing classmate raised an eyebrow. "Uh... hello? Why are you both just... standing here like that?" He waved a hand in front of their blank faces, then repeated louder, "Helloooo?? Can you guys hear me??" Still, neither responded.

Finally, as if a switch flipped, the two girls snapped out of it at the exact same moment. Kavya coughed awkwardly. "Hmm... sorry, sorry. Hallucinated for a second." They slipped quietly into their seats, still rattled, still staring at the glowing phone. Neither dared to say it out loud, but both knew they were thinking the same thing: Did Vishwa just message what we think he messaged?

The Warning

chapter 7
The Warning

Still dazed from what had just happened, Thinovika and Kavya sat on the last bench, trying hard to pretend they were just "normal students." Kavya kept nudging her with her elbow, whispering nervously for her to say something, but Thinovika remained silent, lost in thought. Before she could even gather herself, the classroom door creaked open. Heavy footsteps followed, and in walked someone unexpected — not a faculty member, not even a fellow student from their year, but the final-year representative.

He carried himself with an air of authority, his ID tag swinging as he walked, his expression set in stone. He stopped at the front of the class and faced everyone like a strict warden about to deliver a verdict. His voice cut through the room, stern and unyielding. He said he would keep it short, then added that he knew some students had been running meme pages. The words were sharp, his tone anything but playful. Nervous laughter rippled across the room, but he remained dead serious.

The warning was clear: no offensive posts, no targeting, and no crossing the line. The room fell into heavy silence, every student suddenly aware of the weight in his words. Kavya's breath caught in her throat as his eyes scanned across the room, lingering for just a second too long on their bench. It wasn't an accusation, but it felt dangerously close to one.

He repeated that this wasn't a threat, only a heads-up, and spoke of people who had landed in real trouble because of such pages. Then, without another word, he left – the tension trailing behind him like static in the air. For a long moment, neither of them moved.

Finally, Thinovika leaned toward Kavya, her voice barely above a whisper. "He didn't say it's our page, right?" she asked, her tone uneasy. Kavya's reply came slowly, almost hesitantly. "No... but I think he knows. Or someone does."

And just like that, the pressure around their secret began to rise, heavier than before.

While they were still giggling, Kavya's phone buzzed first. It was only a group chat, and she rolled her eyes in mild annoyance. A second later, Thinovika's phone chimed with a different tone. She picked it up casually, but the moment her eyes scanned the screen, she froze.

Kavya leaned closer, suspicion flickering across her face. "Aiyo... don't tell me it's—" Thinovika cut her off with a mischievous smirk. "Guess who just slid into my DMs?" Kavya's eyes widened in disbelief. "No. Noooo. Don't tell me it's Vishwa." The truth hit her almost instantly, her chest tightening as though she had been caught in the blast of a secret. Thinovika, still grinning like she had pulled off a clever trick, confirmed softly, "Yeah. It's from Vishwa."

Before Thinovika could say more, Kavya snatched the phone from her hand, her voice rising with urgency. "What did he say? WHAT?" Her eyes darted across the screen, bracing herself for the worst. But the message wasn't an accusation, not even a threat.

It was simple. Just: Hey admin. Followed by a meme—about the admin herself.Thinovika leaned back, smiling like a cat who knew it held the advantage. "He just sent... a meme. About me. Well... about the admin."
Kavya blinked, half shocked, half impressed. "Wait, wait, wait... he's trying to flirt with the enemy?"
"Looks like it," Thinovika replied smoothly, her confidence radiating. "Poor guy doesn't know he's playing chess with the queen."

Kavya shot her a wary smile. "Or maybe... the queen's about to be checkmated."Thinovika stretched back in her seat, her smirk deepening. "We'll see. Game's on."Both of them broke into an evil little laugh, mischief and tension crackling in the air. Yet beneath it all, just for a fleeting second, a thin layer of fear remained—small, but undeniable.

Late at night, both of them sat online, their screens glowing with an odd mix of curiosity and hesitation. Thinovika was the first to break the silence, her reply teasing and light —"Me?? Who??"—to which Vishwa immediately responded with a challenge: he wanted to ask her questions, just yes or no answers, nothing more. She agreed, amused, and he reminded her it had to be the truth, to which she shot back confidently that he could trust her blindly. His first question landed: was she a member of their crew? Her answer came quick and sharp—absolutely not.

Vishwa blinked at the screen, surprised, because he was certain she was. He told her as much, only for her to reply that she wished she was, but she didn't have talents like them. Still trying to trap her, Vishwa asked which department she belonged to and even joked he would block her if she didn't answer, but Thino only added to the mystery, hinting she wasn't in Civil or Mechanical yet refusing to say directly.

Vishwa frowned, confused, convinced she would be from one of those. He typed again, questioning her truth, and she only laughed it off, swearing she didn't like to lie and loved—then paused. Vishwa leaned in closer, eager, and asked what she loved. Her answer arrived sly and playful: she loved playing with people's curiosity.

Vishwa nearly dropped his phone, shocked at her boldness, and covered it with a laughing emoji before admitting she was dangerous. Thino grinned and reminded him he was still talking to her anyway, while inside she was cringing at how awkward the auto-correct had made her words. Vishwa, meanwhile, leaned back, baffled that he still couldn't figure out who she really was, but despite the confusion, he found himself laughing. He liked her—at least that's what he thought, though he tried to convince himself it wasn't her meme page that drew him in.

Yet even as he reasoned with himself, the thought slipped in: maybe he simply liked her. Both kept typing and deleting, the blinking dots on the screen betraying their hesitation, the words unsent but heavy in the silence, leaving the night suspended in unspoken tension and delicious curiosity.

Text and Clash

chapter 8
Text and Clash

Thino had been posting pictures of their crew from time to time, and somehow, without realizing it, most of them ended up being of him—her camera roll had slowly turned into a gallery that was eighty percent Vishwa's face. One evening, when she opened her secret page, another message from him popped up. Her heart skipped. Oh my god, Thino, calm down... act normal. Vishwa had simply typed, "Hello... thanks for your support ma." She forced herself to sound casual, replying, "That's my pleasure, senior." Then, with a smirk she couldn't hide even from herself, she added, "Is there any talk about me in your crew?" To her shock, Vishwa answered, "Yeah... there is. How did you know that?" Thino teased, "I have my people and spies to watch." "Watch??? Whom?" he pressed.

Panic flickered as she slipped, "Watch college..." and immediately regretted saying it. Vishwa only laughed, replying, "Ma... you are really really dangerous." "You think so?" she typed with a grin. Then, half-joking, she asked, "Can I join your crew? I don't have any talent... so cleaner or watchwoman would also be fine." He dismissed it gently: "Oh goodness... no need of that. You can simply come and learn also." She protested, "But I can't... crew members should know about music la." Vishwa, unbothered, replied, "Then visit on evenings ma." Her heart fluttered. This man... if he talks like this, I think I'll fall for him.

"You're trapping me, senior," she teased again. "Trap? This is called invitation," he shot back. "Invitation to fall into trouble ah?" she challenged. "Maybe... depends on how much trouble you bring." Thino smirked, "I can bring a lot." Vishwa countered coolly, "That's why I said 'visit'... not 'join.'" She gasped, "Wow... insult in style." "Not insult, ma... warning," he corrected. "Now I really want to come," she replied, excitement slipping through her tone. "Then come. Simple." "Okay fine... but if I faint seeing your crew's talent, you're responsible." "Deal," he promised, before adding, "But if you faint, I'm posting it on my status." Thino giggled at the screen and typed, "Senior... I think I'll bring chilli powder for safety." Vishwa responded instantly, "Dangerous spy indeed." She laughed out loud in the quiet of her room, clutching the phone. This man... if I keep texting him like this, one day, I'm going to give myself away.

That day, the weather hardly mattered because Thinovika and Kavya were too busy laughing at some silly meme they had seen earlier, lost in their own world of jokes. As they walked into the first-year block, fate seemed to play its favorite trick again – almost colliding head-on with Vishwa. She froze, and for a split second, so did he. Her eyes automatically turned toward him in slow motion, her heart thundering inside her chest as though it wanted to expose her feelings. Don't beat this fast, you idiot, you'll make it obvious, she scolded herself silently. But Vishwa? He walked away without a second thought – calm, collected, completely unbothered – while her heart continued to play dhol beats in chaos.

Kavya, already giggling at the sight, leaned in and whispered teasingly, "Girl... this is getting suspicious." Thinovika, unable to ignore the heaviness in her chest, pulled out her phone a few minutes later and sent him a message: Soo... senior... you visited our block today, huh? Vishwa replied almost instantly, Hey... are you the girl I saw a few minutes ago?

Her heart skipped a beat. He knows! Play it cool, Thino, play it cool, she told herself before typing back, Me? Nooo... I was in my classroom actually... why? Vishwa's next message came calmly: Nothing... just thought I saw someone familiar. She teased, Familiar? I doubt it... unless you have secret spy cameras in our block. His answer, Who knows... maybe I do, left her stunned. Oh my God, why is this man casually dangerous?! she thought, before silence stretched between them and both went offline. But that night, when Vishwa picked up his phone again, a new notification blinked on his screen. He opened it and froze. The words stared back at him: I'm Thinovika from the ECE department... I'm the admin. Shock flooded him as he whispered under his breath, Wait... WHAT?!

The First Handshake

chapter 9
The First Handshake

Hours before that shocking confession, Thinovika and Kavya were walking toward the hostel meeting hall, their steps heavy with unease. Kavya whispered, almost angrily, that some girl was being blamed for running the meme page. Thinovika was stunned. How could they blame someone without proof? Kavya shook her head, explaining that the girl didn't even know how to edit photos. The irritation in Thinovika's chest grew as they entered the room.

The air smelled faintly of chai and damp curtains, the floor packed with girls sitting cross-legged, whispering, staring, pretending to scroll through phones but clearly tuned in. And all those eyes, all those whispers, pointed toward one particular girl. Thinovika followed their gaze and saw her — shrinking in discomfort under the weight of judgment. Kavya warned her to stay quiet, but the whispers cut sharper: "Flirting with seniors... cheap things to do... acting innocent." Then a senior muttered, "We all know who's behind the meme page." Something inside Thinovika snapped.

"It's me," she said aloud.

The room froze. Kavya jumped in, panicked, insisting she was joking. But Thinovika's voice didn't waver this time. She admitted it again, facing everyone. Kavya could only stare at her in disbelief – this wasn't the same girl she thought she knew. Thinovika's voice shook, but her words were sharp: yes, she was the admin, but no, she wasn't using it to flirt with seniors or insult staff. "I post memes because it was the only thing that made me laugh here. And you turned it into something dirty." The room grew heavy with silence, broken only when the warden cleared her throat and ended the discussion.

Thinovika sat down, heart racing, hands trembling, but unwilling to show weakness. Kavya, strangely proud, whispered with a small smile, "That's my girl."
What Thinovika didn't know was that some girls had secretly recorded her confession. By night, the blurry video spread across WhatsApp groups – sparking both support and mockery. Sitting in her room, guilt gnawing at her, she messaged Vishwa: "I'm Thinovika from ECE... I'm the admin." Almost immediately, his DM popped up: "Nice speech." Her breath caught.

The club Chairman himself? She tried to deflect – calling it free entertainment – but his reply was steady: "Maybe. Or maybe you just made half of them think twice." When she asked why he was even messaging her, his answer was simple: "You didn't hide. Most people would." She almost smiled. For the first time that day, the burden felt a little lighter.

Behind the scenes, Vishwa had already rallied his crew, working overnight to erase every trace of the video. "Clear it as soon as possible," he ordered. His friends teased him for caring too much, but he brushed it off, restless until it was gone. Thinovika never knew.

By morning, the clips had vanished from every group. Kavya, half-disappointed, sighed, "I thought we'd be famous overnight." Thinovika rolled her eyes. "Enough joking. It's good they're gone." Kavya muttered under her breath, "I lost the chance to be famous." Thinovika narrowed her eyes. "What?" Kavya chuckled quickly. "Nothing, nothing."
It had been a week since the "almost clash," and Thino's heart hadn't quite recovered. During lunch break, Kavya rushed to her with news that sent a fresh wave of panic through her chest — one of her friends had just been selected into Vishwa's crew, and they had been invited to drop by the crew block for orientation. Thino's pulse quickened. That very morning, she had done something she never usually dared to — she wore makeup for the first time and slipped into a soft yellow dress, her curly hair left free and bouncy. But standing at the gate now, she couldn't help second-guessing everything about herself. She muttered that maybe they could go some other time, but Kavya was having none of it; with a playful smack on the arm and a teasing grin, she pulled her along.

And then, at the entrance, there he was. Vishwa stood effortlessly composed in a casual shirt, welcoming the juniors beside his friend. Kavya's friend introduced them, and while Vishwa's friend greeted Thino first with a warm grin, the real test came when Vishwa himself extended his hand. The moment their palms touched, a jolt ran through her, her breath catching as her heartbeat thundered in her ears. Her hand was cold, and she knew he noticed, though he didn't say a word – only that calm, unreadable look of his. Then his friend broke the silence with a laugh, announcing to Vishwa that Thino was the admin of the meme page everyone loved.

Vishwa's lips curved into the faintest smile as he replied, "Ahhh... I didn't know." But his eyes gave him away – he already did.Leaning slightly closer, his voice softened just enough for her to hear. "I love the memes you've been posting. We enjoyed, ma..." The last word echoed in her mind like a melody – ma, ma, ma. She couldn't help the way her eyes lit up, the smile that didn't quite reach her lips but shone unmistakably in her gaze. He noticed. And just like that, something unspoken stirred between them. Meanwhile, Vishwa's friend turned his attention to Kavya, teasing her about being the one always tagged in the memes. Kavya laughed, admitting her guilt, their handshake lingering a little longer than expected, enough to make her arch a brow before smirking knowingly. It was a small moment, almost ordinary to anyone else – yet for both Thino and Kavya, something quietly, undeniably, had begun.

The meeting at the crew block had lasted no more than ten minutes, but for Thino, it felt as if she had endured a two-hour exam without preparation. Her palm still tingled, and she looked at her hand as though it had turned to gold—something precious she wasn't ready to believe belonged to her. Kavya nudged her as they walked out, teasingly asking why she was moving as if she had just touched a celebrity. Thino avoided eye contact, insisting she was walking normally, but her steps betrayed her, light and almost floating. Her mind, however, was lost in a single echoing word—ma. The way Vishwa had said it—soft, casual, yet heavy enough to make her cheeks warm even now—kept replaying in her head.

Kavya's voice pulled her back, accusing her of smiling like a movie heroine in slow motion. Thino muttered for her to shut up, though the smile in her eyes refused to fade. Kavya, always quick to stir mischief, added that Vishwa's friend might actually be more handsome than Vishwa, earning nothing but a sharp glare from Thino. By the time they reached the canteen, Kavya had already shifted focus, pointing out how firmly Vishwa's friend had shaken Thino's hand—without any awkwardness, something she considered rare. Thino brushed it off, calling her weird for noticing, but Kavya only grinned, boldly claiming she thought Vishwa's friend liked her.

Thino shot back with a smirk, asking if he liked her or her unlimited snack coupons, and Kavya shrugged, saying either worked. Their laughter echoed easily between them, but beneath it all, Thino's heart remained elsewhere, lingering in the memory of calm eyes, a steady voice, and that one word—ma—now looping endlessly in her mind, taking root like it belonged there.

The hostel room was unusually quiet that night. Kavya had gone out for a late-night chai run, leaving Thino alone on her bed, still in the soft yellow dress she'd worn earlier. Hours had passed, and though she had meant to change, she couldn't bring herself to take it off yet. Her phone lay beside her, dark and silent. She wasn't scrolling through Instagram or checking notifications; she was simply... waiting. For what, she wasn't entirely sure—or maybe she was.

Her mind kept drifting back to the handshake earlier that day. His hand had been warm, hers hadn't, and she was certain he'd noticed. And that ma... the way he had said it. Every time she thought about it, an uncontrollable, silly smile spread across her face. Then, her phone buzzed. A message. Vishwa: Hey. Thanks for coming today. She stared at it for what felt like thirty seconds, reluctant to seem too eager, before typing back carefully, Thino: Yeah... it was nice meeting you. There was a pause. Three dots appeared, vanished, appeared again. Vishwa: By the way... your memes are good. Like... really good. Makes a lot of us laugh during breaks.

Her heart skipped a beat. She typed a reply, deleted it, typed again, deleted again, until finally settling on Thino: Thanks, ma. She hit send before she could overthink, her cheeks burning. What if he thought she was mocking him? But then... that tiny smile emoji from him was enough to make her heart flutter. She set her phone down, hugged her pillow tightly, and whispered into the quiet room, "Idiot... now I'm never going to sleep."

Operation Follow Vishwa

chapter 10
Operation Follow Vishwa

The early morning hostel was unusually quiet, with only the soft echoes of slippers and the distant creak of doors filling the air. Thino had just splashed water on her face and was brushing her teeth when Kavya burst into the room like a whirlwind, eyes wide with urgency. "Thino! Your phone's ringing!" she exclaimed. Thino, toothbrush mid-air, rolled her eyes lazily. "So? Let it ring, I'm brushing." But Kavya wasn't letting her off the hook. "You... idiot... it's Vishwa."
Time seemed to freeze. Foam barely clinging to her lips, Thino could only manage a stunned, "...Wh-what?? Vishwa? Our Vishwa?" Before she could process, Kavya practically shoved her toward the bed, yanking the toothbrush away and leaving Thino's heart hammering. She grabbed her phone, pressed the answer button, and tried to steady her trembling voice. "H...hello?" she whispered.

Vishwa's voice came through, calm, warm, and with a subtle depth that made her chest flutter. "Hey... this is Vishwa. I hope I'm not disturbing?" Thino blinked, words abandoning her. "N-no... it's fine," she finally managed. "I just wanted to thank you... that video you made for the seniors... it was brilliant. The way you mixed humor with the emotional bit at the end—it made everyone laugh and tear up." Her mind whirled: he had noticed. He liked it. "Hmm... yes... thanks..." she murmured, almost inaudibly.

There was a gentle warmth in his voice as he continued. "I didn't know the admin of the meme page had this side too. You really put a lot of heart into it, I can tell." Thino gripped the bedsheet until her knuckles went pale. Words refused to come. "Hmm... yeah..." she whispered again. Vishwa's voice remained soft, sincere: "No really... it was more than just editing. It had... feeling. That's rare. You should be proud." Her chest tightened painfully, nerves screaming at her to say something, anything. She managed only, "Hmm... thank you..."

A short, low chuckle escaped him. "You're quiet... am I making you nervous?" she stammered. "No... I mean... uh... maybe..." His laugh wrapped around her like a gentle warmth. "I just wanted to say it personally. Not everyone takes the time to do something that thoughtful. So... thank you, Thino." That one utterance of her name—soft, deliberate—made her knees weak. "...Anytime," she whispered, barely audible.

When the call ended, her ears still rang and her heart pounded as Kavya leaned against the doorway, grinning. "Girl... you're gone. Sooo... how did the number magically appear in your contacts already, madam?"

Thino pretended to scroll through her phone. "Uh... I... I might've saved it... you know... just in case of... uh... emergencies." Kavya's finger tapped her chest. "Emergency like... heart attack? Because clearly you just had one when he said 'hello.'" Thino threw a pillow at her in protest. "Shut up! My heart just... skipped a little." Kavya laughed harder. "A little? I could hear it from across the room!" Thino buried her face in her hands, cheeks burning. "It's not my fault, okay? His voice... it's just... ugh..."

Kavya smirked knowingly. "Say it—you're in love with his voice already." Thino shook her head, smiling shyly, trying to argue in her mind: No... not love... I just... appreciate it... musically.

"Musically?" Kavya teased, grinning wider. "You were nodding like a fangirl at a concert. 'Hmm... yes... thanks...' That's all you said! If I didn't know better, I'd think you were talking to your exam invigilator." Thino groaned, face still hidden in her hands. "I didn't know what to say! My brain shut down, okay? His 'hello' fried all my circuits."

Kavya chuckled again. "Next time, at least try not to sound like you're giving one-word answers in a police interrogation." Thino peeked up, shyly smiling. "Fine... I'll... practice." Then, after a soft cough, Kavya asked casually, "But Thino... don't take it wrong, but what do you even see in him? I mean, he's not even that handsome or attractive."

Thino looked down, a faint smile curling her lips, and thought quietly to herself: I saw nothing except him.

The hostel was wrapped in quiet, the kind that made every little sound – a creak, a shuffle, a distant cough – feel amplified. Thino sat on her bed, knees pulled up, phone clutched in her hands. She stared at the chat window, fingers hovering. Hey... typed itself, then vanished. What are you doing? Another deletion. Finally, after several rounds of this internal battle, she settled on something safe, casual: Hi... what's up?

rom the corner of her eye, she saw Pragya watching, a mischievous glint in her eyes. Shalu leaned over next, peeking at the screen. The two friends always knew how to push Thino's buttons, and tonight was no exception.

"Who are you texting at this hour?" Pragya asked, voice dripping with curiosity.

"No one... just... a friend," Thino replied, trying to sound nonchalant.

Shalu's eyes sparkled. "Ohhh. A tall, glasses-wearing, sings-at-club-events kind of friend?"

Thino snorted. "Stop making it sound like that."

"Do you like him?" Pragya asked, leaning in.

Thino froze. "No." A pause. "...Maybe." Another pause. "...I don't know."

The girls exchanged a look that promised trouble.

"Then text him. Tell him," Shalu urged.

Thino immediately shook her head. "No way. Are you crazy? He'll think I'm... I don't know... weird."

Pragya rolled her eyes. "Weird? You run a meme page roasting half the college. You're already weird. Just do it."

Minutes ticked by, each one heavier than the last. Shalu leaned closer. "Come on. It's just words."

Thino's chest tightened. "Exactly. Words that I can never take back."

Finally, after what felt like an eternity, Pragya snatched the phone. "No! No, no, no, give it back–" Thino protested, panic rising in her voice. They laughed, teasing, but returned it.

"Fine," Pragya said. "You type it. We'll shut up."

Thino stared at the screen. Her thumb hovered, heart pounding, stomach knotting with nerves. Slowly, painstakingly, she typed: I think I like you.

She read it three times. Deleted it. Typed it again. Finally... she hit Send. Her phone flew onto the bed as she jumped up, pointing at them. "Okay, it's done. Don't. Touch. My. Phone."

She couldn't sit still, heart racing like a drum. She bolted from the bed, stepping into the hostel corridor for air. The cool night hit her face, and she drew a shaky breath.

Then...

Ding. Her phone buzzed. A call.

Fell In Love After Rejection

chapter 11
Fell In Love After Rejection

The phone rang, sharp and insistent in the quiet of the hostel corridor. Thino froze, her fingers hovering over the screen, then slowly turned it to see the caller ID. Him. Vishwa. Every nerve in her body lit up like a thousand fireworks going off at once. Her heart slammed against her ribs as she finally pressed the answer button. “H...hello...?” she whispered, voice trembling.

Vishwa’s voice came through, calm, deep, weighted in a way that made her sit up straighter, almost as if his tone alone demanded attention. “I got your message. I... I... didn’t expect it, honestly.” He drew a small breath, quieter now, almost like he was speaking to himself. “Thing is,” he continued, words deliberate, soft, “I’ve been in love with someone else. For a long time. Not a month, not a semester... a year. It wasn’t the kind of love you talk about every day. It was the kind where you notice every little thing about someone, even when they don’t notice you exist. The way she tucks her hair behind her ear when she’s reading... how she laughs differently depending on who she’s talking to... how she disappears into her own little world when she’s walking alone. I never told her. Not once. Not because I was scared of rejection—though maybe that too—but because... I believed in knowing someone before loving them openly. And I didn’t know if I was allowed into her world yet. So I stayed on the outside, just... watching from a distance. People say you can’t love someone without being close to them, but I did.

I loved the idea of her, the real her I saw when nobody else was looking. It wasn't about her noticing me. It was about me noticing her."

A pause followed, the faint sound of him shifting, maybe leaning back. "And yeah... I still think about her. That's why, when I got your message, I had to be honest with you. If you like me just because I'm this mysterious club Chairman or because I make you curious, then it's not going to work. I don't do fast. I don't do... crushes that turn into love overnight. I'm old-school—the kind of guy who wants friendship first, connection second, love last. In that order. That's how I fell for her. That's how I'd want to fall for anyone." His tone softened, gentle now, almost like he was trying to cushion the blow.
"So... if this is something real, if it's more than a crush, then time will tell. But if it's just because you think I'm interesting right now... better to know the truth before either of us gets hurt." Silence followed, broken only by her shallow breaths and the faint hum of his in the background. "...Mmm," she murmured. A tiny smile crept into his voice. "Goodnight, Miss Mystery Admin." Click.

Thino stared at her phone, his words echoing in her head. The quiet of the room felt heavier now, charged with the weight of honesty. Pragya, from the bed across, noticed her expression. "Judging by your face, I'm guessing that wasn't a romantic confession," she said. Thino's lips curved into a small, wistful smile. "...He told me he liked someone else. For a year. And that love... between us... won't work."
Shalu sat up, eyes wide. "Wait, WHAT?! And you just... took it?"

“What else should I do?” Thino whispered, voice soft but steady. “He was so... clear. No drama, no false hope.”
Pragya narrowed her eyes, unconvinced. “Hmm. And yet... you’re smiling right now.”
Thino’s gaze dropped. She pressed her face against the pillow, cheeks warming. Actually... I fell in love with him for real.
“Ahhh?” Pragya gasped.
“I love... I just love him... for who he wants to be and for who he is,” she admitted quietly. “...It’s stupid, I know. But the way he talked about love... and the way he loved that girl... it’s real. It’s... rare.”
“So his rejection made you fall for him?” Pragya teased lightly.
Thino’s whisper was barely audible. “...Maybe it gave me a reason to.” Her friends exchanged glances, half-amused, half-concerned. Thino turned away, lying back on her pillow. The ceiling fan hummed softly above, the darkness of the room wrapping around her like a cocoon.
In the quiet of her mind, she thought: He doesn’t want me. But somehow... I’ve never wanted someone more. Not because he’s perfect... but because he’s real. And that’s scarier than any love story I’ve ever known.
The college canteen buzzed with chatter and the clatter of trays, but Thino barely noticed. She sat alone at a corner table, scrolling through her phone with a faintly dreamy expression, as if the rest of the world existed only in the background.

Kavya appeared moments later, tray of samosas in hand, and plopped down beside her with a dramatic flourish. “Okay, spill,” she demanded, eyes glinting with mischief. “Pragya told me you had some intense late-night call with Vishwa yesterday.”

Thino gave her the deadpan stare she reserved for exasperating friends. “It wasn’t intense. It was... educational,” she said, her voice flat.

Kavya raised a skeptical eyebrow. “Educational? Girl, I thought this was just a crush thing. You weren’t actually gonna confess.”

Thino snorted, scrolling with one finger. “Confess? Please. I didn’t write him a love letter with scented ink and background violin music. I just told him I have a crush on him.”

“That’s basically a confession!” Kavya said, leaning back, arms crossed but still amused.

“No,” Thino corrected firmly, “a confession is ‘I love you, let’s run away and adopt twelve cats.’ What I did was... more like informing a citizen about a pothole in their street. Polite, casual, and completely non-threatening.”

Kavya laughed so hard she nearly dropped her samosa. “Right. And how did this ‘pothole inspection’ go?”

Thino lifted a hand, resigned. “He rejected the proposal for road construction.”Kavya choked mid-bite, nearly spitting out her samosa. “So you’re telling me... you gave him the map, he said, ‘nah, I’ll take the scenic route,’ and you’re still into him?”

Thino shrugged, a faint smile tugging at her lips. "Listen, it's not my fault. His honesty was... annoyingly attractive. Like those minimalistic furniture designs you know you can't afford but still pin on Pinterest."

"You need help," Kavya said, shaking her head.

"I know," Thino admitted, voice softening. "But in my defense, I've upgraded my crush from 'aww, cute guy' to ugh, responsible, emotionally stable man."

Kavya blinked. "You make it sound like you're talking about a washing machine."

"Exactly," Thino said with mock seriousness. "Durable, reliable, low drama... just needs regular maintenance and occasional attention."

Both of them burst into laughter, their voices echoing across the corner of the canteen. From the other side of the table, Shalu, who had been eavesdropping, called out, grinning. "So basically... you didn't confess. You just... advertised."

Thino smirked, leaning back in her chair. "Precisely. And the customer refused to buy. But hey, window shopping is still fun."

Secret Agent

chapter 12
Secret Agent

The hostel room was dim, the soft glow of Thino's laptop illuminating her focused face as she sat cross-legged on her bed, earphones in, surrounded by folders labeled Club Day 2023, Random Snaps, and suspiciously, Vishwa 1, Vishwa 2. Pragya peered over her shoulder, eyes wide. "Why do I feel like you're hacking into NASA right now?" she teased, while Shalu raised an eyebrow, curious about the "illegal mission." Thino barely looked up, a small grin on her lips, replying, "Mission: Project Vishwa," as she trimmed clips of him laughing, playing guitar, speaking at events, and one rare candid of him gazing thoughtfully out a window.

The two friends giggled, teasing her about stalking and fan edits, while Thino concentrated on creating an appreciation post, not just for the meme page but for the way he quietly brightened everything around him. Hours later, she hit upload, the montage set to soft music with the caption: "Some people just light up the room without even trying." Comments poured in—"Damn he's cute ", "Campus crush confirmed ", but when her phone buzzed, it was Vishwa, sending a DM that made her heart skip: "Hey... I just wanted to say thank you. I know you put a lot of effort into that video. The time you spent on it... that matters to me." Thino read it repeatedly, her chest tightening as Pragya and Kavya hovered, squealing softly, teasing and cheering, while Shalu smirked knowingly.

Holding the phone to her chest, Thino whispered to herself, smiling shyly, “Even if he doesn’t like me back... he sees what no one else does,” feeling warmth bloom inside her as Vishwa’s acknowledgment wrapped around her like a quiet, glowing hug.
Late in the evening, the hostel room was quiet, dimly lit by Thino’s phone and laptop screens. She lay sprawled on her bed, scrolling through her meme page analytics while Pragya and Shalu quietly worked nearby. Days had passed, and though everyone assumed she had moved on from the whole “Vishwa” situation, Thino was quietly observing him, maybe a little obsessively, though in her mind it was purely educational. She hid behind pillars, snapping candid shots of him laughing with friends, zooming in on his hands while he fixed things, capturing those fleeting half-smiles that no one else noticed.

Shalu peeked over her shoulder, noticing yet another picture of Vishwa. “Oye... why do I see his face again?” she asked. Thino defended herself immediately, “I’m... collecting data. For a meme. Educational purpose.” Pragya laughed, teasing, “Ah yes, ‘National Geographic: Vishwa in his Natural Habitat’ edition.” After days of careful observation, Thino spent hours at night editing the clips into a warm, genuine video set to soft music—no sarcasm, no teasing, just sincere admiration. When she finally posted it anonymously on her meme page, her heart thumped quietly in anticipation.

Later that night, her phone buzzed. Vishwa: "Hey... did you make that?" She typed back cautiously, "Why?" He replied, "Because it felt... personal. Like it wasn't just some random edit." Thino hesitated: "...Maybe." Then came his words that made her heart leap: "Thank you so much for putting that much effort into it. The time you spent... matters to me." Everyone else commenting on the video only saw his face, calling him cute or photogenic, but he had seen her effort. Thino smiled faintly, clutching her phone. Pragya and Shalu noticed and exchanged knowing glances, teasing her silently. Meanwhile, Vishwa scrolled through Instagram, stopping on the video, rewatching it slowly, noticing the little things—the clip of him smiling, tying a banner, handing a pen to someone—and a realization dawned on him. "Whoever made this... knows things I didn't think anyone saw. Everyone else commented 'handsome' or 'cute,' but this... was effort. And someone cared enough to spend their time on me." Back in the hostel, Pragya nudged Thino, "Okay... explain that smile." Thino, blushing, muttered, "He... noticed my work." Shalu grinned, "And?" Thino shrugged, "And nothing." Pragya leaned closer, smirking knowingly, "Girl, that's not a 'nothing' smile. That's a 'marriage hall is booked in my head' smile." Thino threw a pillow at her, groaning, "Shut up."

The chat between Thino and Vishwa unfolded like a carefully choreographed dance, each message carrying teasing tension and unspoken feelings.

Round one started casually, with Thino typing, “You know, if you weren’t this handsome, I wouldn’t waste my time.” Vishwa’s quick reply—“And yet, you are wasting your time.”—made her groan, yet she couldn’t help curling her lips into a smile as she fired back, “Wasting? No. I’m investing.”

He didn’t reply immediately, and in that silence, he imagined her smirk, confident, maybe too confident, and found that her “investing” comment lingered longer than expected.

Round two escalated the stakes: “Okay, fine, I like you. I really like you. The kind of like where I stalk your WhatsApp DP to see if it changed.” Vishwa feigned alarm, “That’s... mildly concerning,” but she could tell he liked the attention, and privately, he admitted he checked her DP too.

In round three, Thino tried to break through his walls. “So, what’s the real reason you’re rejecting me?” she asked. Vishwa’s calm, rational reply—“Because relationships need more than attraction. They need timing, compatibility... and I’m not looking for that right now.”—was met with her persistent, almost desperate, declaration: “Then I’ll just wait for the world to end and... even when you reject me 10,000 times, I will try one more time because I... love... you... more than myself.” He almost laughed at her audacity, but there was something about her persistence that made it hard to stay cold.

Round four brought playful teasing: "Did you know persistence is sexy?" she typed. Vishwa fired back, "So is leaving people alone." Her response, "Too bad. I'm the first one," accompanied by a wink emoji and a follow-up, "One day you'll thank me for not giving up," made him sigh—not irritated, but curious, wondering how far she would actually go.

Finally, in round five, Thino tried for a serious breakthrough: "Okay, serious question. What would it take for you to say yes?" Vishwa's measured answer—"Patience. A lot of it."—was met with her bold, fearless reply: "Lucky for you, I've got a lifetime." She hit send, heart hammering, while on his side, Vishwa stared at the message, uncertain if she was joking or serious, but secretly enjoying the relentless, persistent, and utterly charming rhythm of their conversation.

Love Sight

chapter 13
Love Sight

The college auditorium buzzed with restless energy as students scrambled for seats, the chatter dimming only when the MC's voice boomed through the speakers: "And next up, Vishwa from the Music Club will be performing for us!" Thino, gripping her friend Kavya's arm, whispered urgently, "Shh, this is the main event. Don't talk to me for the next five minutes, I'm... spiritually occupied." Kavya rolled her eyes, smirking, "You're spiritually obsessed." As the lights dimmed, Vishwa strode onto the stage, adjusting the mic, and Thino's heart practically stopped. Is it possible to get a heart attack from someone just clearing their throat? Asking for a friend. The friend is me. Vishwa's voice carried effortlessly as he announced, "This one's for people who believe in love stories starting in the most unexpected places." Thino's mind instantly raced: Like the random meme post I made about club Chairmans? Oh my God, does he know? Kavya nudged her, whispering, "Stop smiling like that, people are looking." Thino waved her off, murmuring, "I'm just... appreciating music." Kavya teased back, "Appreciating the musician, you mean." Meanwhile, Vishwa scanned the audience, his gaze landing briefly on Thino in the third row, noting the familiar mix of amusement and admiration—or was it mockery? Their eyes met for a fleeting second before she quickly looked down at her phone, pretending to record, cleverly pointing the camera away from him. A small, knowing smile tugged at his lips.

At the college fest, Vishwa was on stage tuning his guitar while Thino "helped" with the sound check, crouched near the mic cord as if handling a priceless artifact. When the sound guy prompted, "Hey, can you test the mic, Vishwa?" he complied, "Testing... one... two..." and Thino whispered to herself, "Ten out of ten..." Vishwa glanced at her curiously. "Hm?" she said quickly, "I said the mic sounds fine!" He couldn't help but think, Why is she suddenly into volunteering for events she's not even part of? And why is she holding the mic cord like it's an ancient relic that belongs in a museum?

Later, during the open mic night, Vishwa's performance ended to polite applause, but Thino wasn't done. She clapped enthusiastically, chanting, "Wooohooo! Encore!" Everyone turned to look at her, and Kavya groaned, "You're embarrassing me." Thino shrugged, "I'm supporting the arts!" Vishwa, still on stage, smiled, amused. "Guess we have a very passionate audience member tonight." Thino's thoughts raced: If you smile like that again, I'm sending you my therapist's bill.

And in the quiet of his mind, Vishwa admitted, She's bold. Either she really likes my music... or she's just messing with me. And honestly, I'm not sure which one scares me more.

Thino scrolled through Instagram, finally landing on Vishwa's profile via the college club page, and nervously tapped the DM button. She typed, deleted, typed again, and eventually sent: "Nice singing today. I mean... nice mic handling. I mean—okay, bye." Two hours later, his reply popped up: "Thanks... I guess?" Thino's fingers flew over the keyboard: "You guess? So you're not sure if you sang nicely?" Vishwa hesitated, then answered cautiously: "Not sure if you meant it or if you're being sarcastic." With a mischievous grin, she shot back, "Why not both?" Vishwa stared at the chat, torn between laughing and running away, caught off guard by her unpredictable charm.

Later that night, past one in the morning, her DM lit up again: "Do you have any idea how annoying it is that your voice is stuck in my head?" Vishwa's reply was dry, almost incredulous: "...You're texting me at 1 am to complain?" Thino didn't miss a beat. "Yeah. Also, do you do birthday parties? Weddings? Divorce celebrations?" He shook his head, typing slowly: "Pretty sure this is harassment." She shot back, teasing, "Only the romantic kind." For a moment, silence. Then Vishwa's thoughts intruded: Do you really love me though I don't love you? She typed back, flustered but earnest: "Hey... what are you even talking about? Of course I will... I'm doing that even now?" He asked again, "Now??" "Yes... I'm in love even if you are not... wait... then you love me. Ahhh!!" Vishwa set the phone down, smiling despite himself, caught between exasperation and amusement.

From his perspective, she was chaos incarnate—unpredictable, teasing, flattering, and mischievous all at once. She sent random memes at odd hours, about singers and stolen hearts, and he had no idea how to respond.

The next time they met in person, at another college event, Thino leaned casually against a table. “Hey rockstar, planning to break any more hearts on stage?” Vishwa shot back with mock confidence, “Not unless you’re volunteering yours.” The words hung between them, charged and electric. Thino’s eyes widened, her inner voice triumphantly whispering, Gotcha. Meanwhile, Vishwa’s mind raced: I’m in trouble.

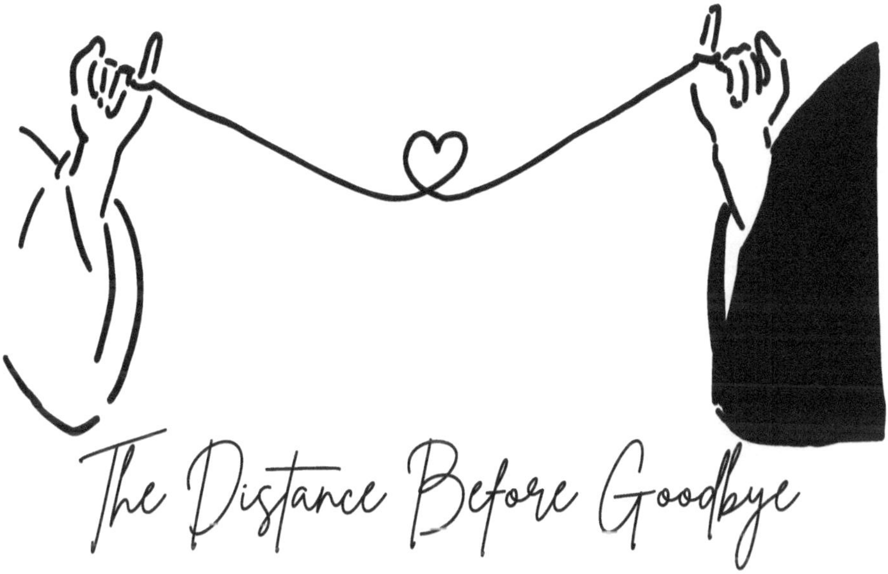

The Distance Before Goodbye

chapter 14
The Distance Before Goodbye

Vishwa sat on the edge of his hostel bed, carefully organizing music sheets for an upcoming performance, when his phone buzzed with a message from Thino: "Don't forget to save me a seat tomorrow." His chest tightened at the sight of her words. She was always there—cheering, laughing, believing in him—but not her, the one he was still waiting for, the one who never came back. With a heavy sigh, he set the phone aside, choosing not to reply immediately.

Weeks slipped by in the same quiet rhythm. Thino's messages came, gentle but probing: "You've been distant lately. Did I do something?" Vishwa's answer was clipped: "No. Just... busy." She pressed further: "Busy avoiding me?" and his brief response, "...I'm not avoiding you," carried the weight of unspoken truths. She let it go, sensing the space he kept between them, though her heart knew otherwise.

One late evening in the campus garden, she found him beneath the old neem tree, alone and pensive. "Vishwa. What's going on? You used to talk to me every day," she asked, her voice steady but searching. He looked up, a shadow of sorrow in his eyes. "...Thino, I don't want to hurt you," he admitted. "Then don't. Just be honest," she urged. His words came slow, deliberate, each one landing like a stone: "I like you... a lot. You're funny, supportive, and one of the best people I've met here. But I'm not in love with you. My heart... it's still somewhere else. I'm still waiting for someone. I can't pretend I feel something I don't."

Her laughter was soft, tinged with sadness, her eyes glistening. "So... that's it? You just close the chapter like that?" she whispered. "It's the only fair thing to do. If I stay, I'll just give you false hope," he replied, voice steady but heavy. She smiled faintly through the ache, murmuring, "You know, I could have loved you enough for both of us." He only shook his head, whispering, "...I'm sorry." Without another word, she walked away, leaving him in the half-light, the sound of her footsteps fading into the night, a quiet reminder that his care was real—but love, for now, belonged elsewhere.

Vishwa sat alone in the quiet club room after the meeting had ended, the chatter and footsteps of his team long gone. His gaze drifted to the whiteboard, cluttered with scribbled schedules, before landing on a water bottle left forgotten by the marker stand. A simple name sticker caught his eye—hers. Her name. She was a junior to him, but somehow always seemed senior in presence, bustling around, lighting up every corner of the room without even trying. Memories flashed unbidden: two years ago, a cultural fest, him tuning his guitar backstage while she strode in, clipboard in hand, directing the crew with effortless authority. "You ready? This stage is yours," she had said, smiling at him. He smiled back, and just like that, his heart had chosen. Even now, she laughed freely with everyone, oblivious to the way his eyes followed her, treating him with friendship and trust—but nothing more.

The evening brought them together again in the campus garden, a coincidental meeting that neither had planned. Thino stepped closer, concern etched across her face. “Vishwa... why are you pulling away from me?” she asked softly. He looked down, struggling with the weight of honesty. “...I like you, Thino. You’re one of the best people I’ve met here. But I’m not in love with you.” Her brow furrowed. “So... who is the girl you mentioned before?” he sighed, reluctant but truthful. “...She’s part of the club. A junior to me. Senior to you. I’ve liked her for a long time.” The words hit harder than any rejection she had anticipated. “Does she know?” she whispered. “No. And even if she did... I don’t think she feels the same.” Thino swallowed, the pain settling deep—not because the timing was wrong, but because his heart was already claimed. “... Maybe. But I can’t force my heart somewhere it doesn’t belong,” he admitted quietly. She nodded, a soft, broken smile brushing her lips. “Good luck then,” she murmured, turning away and holding back tears until she disappeared from sight. Vishwa remained on the bench, strumming a chord that never resolved, each note echoing the quiet ache of unspoken feelings.

The semester ended. He left for Chennai for work, and all contact ceased—no messages, no DMs, nothing. Thino struggled to move on, every day a battle between her heart and reality. It was hard—so very hard—but she had no choice. She had to.

Thino's Silence & Kavya's Confrontation

chapter 15
Thino's Silence & Kavya's Confrontation

The hostel room was unusually quiet, a soft hush that seemed almost out of place amidst the usual chaos. The meme group chat buzzed endlessly with notifications, but Thino didn't even glance at her phone. Her laptop sat open, cursor blinking on an unfinished meme template, abandoned, while she lay on her bed staring blankly at the ceiling, lost in the weight of her thoughts. The silence was broken by Kavya, who entered with her usual whirlwind energy, balancing two steaming cups of coffee. She froze for a moment, taking in Thino's stillness.

"Ayyo, what's this funeral mood in our room? Did someone die in your imagination, or did our meme page lose followers?" Kavya asked, plopping down beside her. Thino didn't move, her voice barely above a whisper. "Nothing... just tired." Kavya squinted, refusing to accept the excuse. "Don't you dare 'nothing' me. You've been acting like this since yesterday. You didn't even laugh at my 'tea vs. coffee' joke. That's not you. Now talk." Thino's shoulders slumped, and her voice cracked as she finally admitted, "He rejected me, Kavs... sincerely this time. Not in a rude way... but in a way that hurt more. He said he likes me, but... he's still waiting for that girl. I don't know why, but hearing that just... broke something inside."

Kavya put the coffee down and let a serious calm replace her usual mischief. “Listen... I know it hurts. But you’re crying because you loved purely. That’s never wrong. You fell for him with all your heart, not halfway like others. And you know what? That’s your strength, Thino. Not your weakness.” Thino’s eyes shimmered with tears, her voice barely audible. “But why me, Kavs? Why can’t I ever be the one someone chooses first? I gave my time, my efforts... I even made him see sides of me no one else does. And still... I wasn’t enough.” Kavya reached over, gently but firmly taking her hand. “Stop it. You are more than enough. If he doesn’t see it now, that’s his loss. Not yours. One day, someone will see you the way I see you every day – stubborn, dramatic, but also the most genuine soul in this hostel. Till then, you’re stuck with me. So... no more ceiling staring. Drink your coffee.” Thino let out a weak laugh, a tiny spark of relief in the gloom. “You sound like one Tamil serial amma character,” she teased.

“Better that than a silent ghost roommate. Now, sit up. If you don’t laugh in the next two minutes, I’ll upload your old school ID photo on the meme page,” Kavya threatened with mock seriousness. Thino couldn’t help herself–she burst into laughter, shoving Kavya with a pillow, feeling a little lighter despite the ache in her heart.

The Box of Memories

chapter 16
The Box of Memories

The hostel corridors that had once echoed with their laughter now felt unusually heavy, a silent reminder of an era coming to an end. After countless late-night talks, exam cramming sessions, and heart-to-hearts in the narrow confines of their hostel room, Thino and Kavya finally moved out, renting a small room near campus as their first-year college days edged toward their final stretch. The room was modest—two cots, a wooden table, one cupboard, and a small window overlooking the busy street—but to them, it symbolized freedom. Kavya, never one to let a moment pass without humor, dropped her bag dramatically and exclaimed, “Ahh... new room, new life, new vibes! And... hopefully... no late-night sobbing of my roommate over her 'college singer crush’?” Thino rolled her eyes but managed a weak smile. “Shut up, Kavya... I told you, I’m moving on.” Kavya grinned mischievously. “Yeah, yeah, moving on... until he sings on stage again and you melt like butter on dosa.” Thino swatted her with a pillow, but deep down, she knew Kavya wasn’t wrong. Vishwa’s presence lingered in her mind—in his songs, in the corridors where she’d catch glimpses of him laughing with friends, in college events she tried to avoid.

Days bled into weeks. Thino tried to fill her time—assignments, late-night drama binges, evening walks with Kavya—but memories clung like dust that refused to be wiped away. One evening, while cleaning her cupboard, she stumbled upon an old, dusty storage box hidden behind piles of books. Curiosity piqued, she opened it to find a brownish piece of paper, stained with faint coffee marks. Her chest tightened—it was the coffee letter, written in her younger, almost innocent handwriting. The words weren't dramatic; they were soft, like an unspoken whisper of love: "I don't know how to tell you this, so I let the coffee speak instead. Maybe love is just this warm feeling—like the first sip after a long day, like the way your songs fill the emptiness. I don't want to own you, I just want to admire you, quietly. If someday you notice me, I'll consider it my luck. Until then, I'll keep this little piece of love here."
Pressing the letter to her chest, Thino felt the sting of her own past foolishness and innocence. Digging further, she found a small wind chime she had bought with her sister—a simple, silver-threaded creation with tiny bells that sang with the wind.

The memory hit instantly: she had imagined giving it to Vishwa countless times—during club events, casually in the corridor, or perhaps someday while talking about music—but the moment never came. Holding it now, she realized that keeping it meant remembering him over and over. Yet maybe, she thought, it was better this way; he would never know the meaning behind it, but at least it wouldn't haunt her here.

Just then, Kavya entered, carrying two cups of tea. She paused at the sight of Thino sitting on the floor, holding the chime in one hand and the letter in the other, tears quietly rolling down her cheeks. "Found the ghosts, huh?" she asked softly, sitting beside her. Thino nodded, whispering, "I wanted to forget... but these things... they pull me back." Kavya placed a cup near her and said gently, "Then maybe it's time you let them go. Not because he asked you to... but because you deserve to breathe without weight." Thino stared at the chime as a soft breeze tinkled the tiny bells, like a farewell song—light, fleeting, yet beautiful. Taking a deep breath, she spoke slowly, more to herself than to Kavya, "I'll give these to him. Not to win him. Not to remind him of me. Just... so I can finally move on." That night, in the dimly lit room near campus, surrounded by scattered memories, Thino finally made peace with her first love and decided to let go.

The Yellow Dress Evening

chapter 17
The Yellow Dress Evening

The night had weighed heavily on Thino after rediscovering the letter and the wind chime, and just as she tried to settle, her phone lit up—Vishwa's name flashing on the screen. Her heart skipped and then raced; for a fleeting second, she thought her eyes were playing tricks, but no—it was real. "I'm visiting college for some business, let's meet." She read it again and again, her hands trembling, her mind spinning with possibilities. Kavya, noticing her frozen stare, leaned over with a raised brow. "Who's that? Don't tell me it's—" "Vishwa," Thino whispered, cutting her off. Kavya's eyes softened, sensing the spark returning to her friend's face after months of quiet ache, and wisely chose to stay silent.

The next morning, Thino woke with nervous energy, every little motion charged with anticipation—braiding her curls twice, changing outfits three times, checking herself in the tiny mirror repeatedly—until she finally settled on the yellow dress, the same one she had worn the day they first met. Kavya sipped her tea, teasing gently, "Yellow dress... huh. Somebody's carrying a little too much hope today." Thino smiled nervously, whispering, "Don't jinx it, Kavya... maybe today's different." With her heart racing, she left early, walking fast through the bright morning, each step feeling like it was leading her toward something significant. By evening, she arrived near the crew block where Vishwa had asked to meet.

The place buzzed with students, but her focus was entirely on the moment. And then he appeared—calm, confident, his eyes searching. Unknown to Thino, Vishwa had reached out to multiple friends that day, expecting the girl he truly liked to show up. But it was Thino, in her yellow dress, waiting with hopeful anticipation. For a brief moment, something softened in him—the sincerity in her gaze, her quiet nervousness—but he held back, keeping the conversation casual, avoiding any thread that might give false hope. They exchanged small words, updates about college and mutual friends, laughing at minor jokes, yet the space between them remained, weighted with unspoken truths. Eventually, Vishwa excused himself, and Thino, her smile faltering only briefly, watched him walk away, the sunset casting long shadows as the crowd dispersed. That evening became another bittersweet memory—one of recognition, warmth, and unfulfilled longing.

Later, as the night settled, Thino prepared for her final gesture. She held the small paper bag containing her old coffee letter and the wind chime, a gift she had once imagined giving Vishwa long ago. She texted him to meet briefly near the coffee shop, and despite his protests about time, he agreed.

At the shop, Kavya quietly observed Thino's trembling fingers as she placed the bag on the table before Vishwa, her voice soft and cracked as she explained, "I thought of keeping it with me... but then I realized, if I see it every day, I'll keep remembering you. So... it's better if it stays with you." Vishwa looked at the gift, then at her, lips parting slightly as if to speak, but no words came. He simply nodded. Thino whispered her goodbye and walked away with Kavya, the gentle tinkle of the wind chime echoing faintly behind her. Side by side, they walked through the night air in silence, the chapter closing—not how she had dreamed, but the way life had written it, leaving behind both ache and a quiet, enduring grace.

The Letter in the Train

chapter 18
The Letter in the Train

Thino's fingers hovered over the phone for a moment that stretched into an eternity. Her heart pounded, threatening to leap out of her chest, as she stared at Vishwa's name flashing on the screen. After months of silence, after the quiet ache of unspoken words and lingering memories, there it was—his voice, waiting to cross the miles between them. Finally, with trembling hands, she pressed the green button.

"Hello?" she whispered, her voice barely above the hum of the yellow bulb in the room, her nerves making the single word feel fragile and heavy.

On the other end, Vishwa's voice carried a calmness that was unusual, yet beneath it, a weight she hadn't heard before, a sincerity that made her pulse quicken. "Thino... it's me. Can we talk?"

Her heart skipped a beat, and her chest tightened with a mixture of hope, disbelief, and the residual ache of past months. "Y-yes... I mean, of course," she stammered, barely able to steady her voice, emotions tangled between excitement and the cautious caution she had carried for so long.

Vishwa: "I... I read your letter. The wind chime. I don't even know how to say this properly, but... I finally understand."
Thino swallowed hard, clutching the pillow beside her as if it could anchor her, steady her racing heart. "Understand... what?" she asked softly, almost afraid of the answer.
Vishwa's voice wavered slightly, betraying his usual composure. "That you... you've been loving me so purely all this time. And I can't ignore it anymore. Not now. I shouldn't have run before. I was blind to what I had, blind to you."
Thino felt her chest tighten further, tears threatening to spill over, but this time, there was a fragile, hopeful light in her chest amidst the pain. "Vishwa... I... I waited, but I never thought—"

Vishwa interrupted her gently but with urgency in his tone, as if he could barely wait to speak the words he had kept inside. "Don't say anything yet. Just... can I come? Can I see you? I need to... explain, properly."
Her breath hitched, a nervous laugh escaping her lips despite the tension in her chest. "Y-yes... please. Come," she whispered, the words trembling but carrying all the hope she had stored in her heart for months.

Kavya, sitting quietly by the window, watched the scene unfold silently, a knowing smile tugging at her lips. She could feel the tide turning, the long-suppressed emotions beginning to rise and shift, as the past and present converged in this quiet moment.

The heavy silence of their rented room lifted slightly, replaced with anticipation and a tender, nervous electricity that filled every corner. Thino clutched the phone to her chest, feeling Vishwa's presence in each word he spoke, imagining his footsteps approaching. Outside, the evening air whispered softly through the half-open window, carrying with it the faint sounds of the bustling street below. And in that small room, with the yellow bulb casting its warm, flickering glow, a chapter that had been waiting in silence, held in memories and quiet longing, finally began to write itself anew, fragile, uncertain, yet beautifully alive.

Thino sat up straight. "No way." Kavya, almost snatching the phone from her hands, exclaimed, "Da, pick up! What if he forgot to give you your wind chime back?" Thino glared at her. "Shut up, idiot." Her hands were trembling slightly as she pressed the green button. Meanwhile, Vishwa sat in the train coach, the gentle sway matching his racing heartbeat. His bag was open beside him, the letter carefully unfolded, and the wind chime hung faintly against the window bar, chiming softly whenever the wind passed. Her words replayed in his head, raw and earnest: "I don't know why I'm writing this... maybe because words will outlive my courage. Maybe you'll never even care. But every time you sang, it felt like the world pressed pause just for me. And that... that was enough." Vishwa smiled helplessly. She really meant every word.

Earlier, his friend Arav had called. Vishwa had confessed everything—about the letter, the chime, Thino. Arav hadn't hesitated: "Machan, the girl literally wrote her heart out, and you're still waiting for someone who doesn't even look at you? Dei, don't be a fool. Go get her." So Vishwa did the one thing he never thought he'd do. He called.

"Hey... reached hostel?" he asked softly. Thino, still stunned, replied, "Uh... yeah. You? Train left?" Vishwa said, "Yeah... train left. But my mind didn't. It's still with that letter." Silence. Kavya's eyes widened, mouthing, "He read it!" Thino's heart pounded as she pretended calm. "Oh... just throw it away. It's old nonsense," she whispered. Vishwa chuckled. "If that's nonsense, then I've been searching for sense in the wrong places." Her breath caught.

He never spoke like this. "You know, everyone always tells me I sing well, or I look confident on stage... but that letter, it didn't see me. It saw my effort, my hours of practice, my character, silly fears. No one noticed that... except you." Thino, trying to lighten the mood, said, "So basically, I'm a CCTV camera." Vishwa laughed loudly, startling nearby passengers. "Yes, exactly. A CCTV that not only records but also... understands." Kavya whispered, excited, "He's flirting da, HE'S FLIRTING." Thino waved her hand dismissively. Vishwa continued, "You know what's funny? When I saw you today in that yellow dress... I remembered the first time I saw you in college. You were standing in front of me, full of nervous... Somehow, I noticed you." Thino stiffened. "Really? I thought you never cared." Vishwa admitted, "I thought so too.

But today, when I expected... someone else, and you came instead, I realized maybe my expectations were wrong all along and..." Thino blinked. Someone else? But she didn't dare ask. "I mean... who buys a wind chime for someone? That too remembering which one I'd like?" he added. Thino murmured, "Someone who's stupid enough to love you." Vishwa gently replied, "Then maybe I need that kind of stupidity in my life." Her heart skipped. Was he...? Impossible.

Vishwa added, almost teasing, "Hmm... I'm actually short-tempered. Is that okay for you?" Thino stammered, "Ahhh??" "I will always be working in music like a psycho. That's not a problem?" he asked. Thino, internally screaming, thought, What's he actually thinking? "Wait wait... are you drunk or what?" she asked. Vishwa grinned. "I don't drink. But maybe your letter is a stronger shot than anything." Thino said, "Ahhhh. You're just guilty. Tomorrow you'll forget this." Vishwa replied, "If I forget, I'll hang the chime outside my window. It'll ring every morning and remind me." Kavya buried her face in a pillow, whispering, "PAAAHHH... THIS IS CINEMATIC."

The call stretched for hours. They talked about silly things—favorite food (she mocked him for loving lemon rice), childhood memories (he teased her about her obsession with collecting stickers), and dreams (she wanted to travel, he wanted to sing abroad). But in between, his words slipped out, truths disguised as jokes.

"You're the only one I feel relaxed texting without thinking too much. With others, I calculate. With you, I just... am," he confessed. "That's because I tolerate your lame emojis," she replied. "No... it's because you tolerate me," he said, making her smile freeze. Did he just—?

It was nearly 2 AM. Kavya had dozed off. Thino sat curled up, the phone pressed close to her chest. "So... why did you really call?" she asked. Vishwa paused. Didn't she get it? She could hear the faint chime in the background. "Because I couldn't sit on this train, reading that letter, and not tell you that it mattered. That you matter. More than you think," he said softly. Her eyes welled up. "See? You're quiet. Maybe I said too much. But that's okay... sometimes I'm scared too," he added lightly. "No... I'm just... not used to hearing it. From you," she whispered. "Can I ask you one thing?" he said. "Yeah..." "Why me?" "Hmm... because I fell in love with your soul before I could ever touch your skin."
For the first time, the silence between them wasn't awkward. It was full. That night, they didn't say "I like you." But he said everything around it. In laughter, in teasing, in pauses. And for the first time, Thino fell asleep with hope again—while Vishwa, watching the chime sway in the train, smiled like a man who had finally found what he'd been blind to all along.

The long call finally ended, Vishwa's voice on the other side soft and gentle. "It's really late, Thino. You should sleep now. I'll... I'll call you tomorrow. Bye." Thino's mind froze for a moment. Tomorrow? Did he just say tomorrow? As in... another call? Her heart leapt like it had run a marathon. This was nothing like their usual dry, short, formal conversations. Today, there was warmth. Murmuring to herself, she whispered, "Tomorrow...? What does that even mean? Why tomorrow?!" The call ended, and she lay back on her bed, hugging her pillow tightly, a thousand thoughts swirling in her mind. Is he teasing? Or is he...? No, no, impossible. Don't even think, Thino. Don't even have little hope. Mental health is more important, isn't it? But he actually spoke like he likes me... no, just shut everything and sleep...

Just as she was about to drift off, her phone buzzed. A notification popped up: 1 new message – Vishwa. Her half-asleep eyes flew open. Trembling hands unlocked the phone. The message read: "I love you. I couldn't say this on call." For a moment, her brain froze, her heart skipped a beat, then pounded harder than ever. Gasping, she sat upright. "Whatttttttttttttttt??!!" she whispered, reading it over and over again. Pinching her arm to confirm she wasn't dreaming, she did it again and again until her skin turned red, but the words glowed on the screen: I. Love. You.

She pressed her face into her pillow, screaming silently before her whispers turned into loud cries. “No way, no way, no way, no wayyy. Vishwa?! Did Vishwa just...?!” Her scream erupted. “Aaaaaaaaaaaaaa!” Kavya, jolted awake in the next bed, groaned. “Thino! What’s wrong? Did you see a ghost?” Thino leapt onto her bed, shaking her friend. “Kavyaaaa! Forget ghosts, this is worse—no, better—no, everythingggg!” She shoved the phone into Kavya’s hands. Squinting and rubbing her eyes, Kavya’s jaw dropped. “No... wait. WHAT?! He texted this?!”

Thino clutched her pillow and screamed into it, “Yes! It’s real. It’s here. Pinch me, pinch meeeeee!!” Kavya pinched her hard enough to make her yelp. “Ow!! Not that hard!” Thino protested, but Kavya was still in shock. “This can’t be... maybe it’s a mistake. Like he meant it for someone else... oh god, what if he meant that girl he liked before?!” Thino held the phone tighter. “Shut up!! Don’t ruin this, Kavyaaa!” Her eyes shimmered with tears—half fear, half joy. “But... what if...? No. No. He wrote my name at the top of the chat. He knows.”
Kavya stared at her, still dizzy with shock. “I swear, I feel half dead reading this. I don’t know whether to faint, scream, or call an ambulance for you.” Thino laughed through tears. “I already died and came back three times since I saw it.” Silence fell for a moment, then both girls locked eyes and burst into hysterical laughter. Thino hugged Kavya tightly. “Kavvuuu... tell me I’m not dreaming... tell me this is real...” Kavya hugged her back softly. “It’s real, Thino. It’s right there in black and white. He loves you.”

Thino pressed the phone to her chest, staring at the ceiling, a smile stretching uncontrollably across her face. Her mind whispered, Out of everyone, me? He chose me? I'm the luckiest girl alive. That night, Thino didn't need sleep—she already had her dream in her hands.

The Gang Knows

chapter 19
The Gang Knows

Thino finally drifted into sleep past 4 a.m., her phone clutched tightly to her chest. When her alarm buzzed at 7, she woke with a jolt—half afraid that last night had been a dream. Her fingers fumbled for the phone, and as the screen lit up, her heart skipped a beat. A new message. From him.

Vishwa: Good morning, Thino. I reached Chennai. Text me back in free time.

Thino whispered to herself, barely able to breathe, "He... messaged again. Morning... like we're already... something." Her lips curved into the widest smile, eyes sparkling, as she read it three times, pressing the phone against her heart and rolling side to side on the bed like a teenager in a rom-com.

Kavya, still half-asleep, pulled the blanket over her head. "Why are you giggling like a lunatic at 7 a.m.? Did your crush send you free breakfast or what?"

Thino sat up dramatically, holding her phone like a holy scripture. "Better than breakfast. He sent me a good morning. And he is no more a crush, got promoted to boyfriend."

Kavya squinted through the blanket, deadpan. "Wow. Revolutionary. Boys texting good morning is the next Nobel Prize material."

Thino, ignoring her, murmured dreamily, “But it’s not just good morning. He added... ‘Text me back in free time.’ That means... he wants to talk. He’s waiting. He cares.”
Kavya threw a pillow at her. “Or maybe he’s just polite, dumbo!” Then, smirking, she added, “But okay, admit it—you’re already dead and reborn in his name.”
Thino hugged her pillow, hiding her face, cheeks burning. “I don’t even know how to reply. If I say just good morning, it’ll sound boring. If I add an emoji, will I look desperate? Ughhh!”
Kavya teased, “Send him your entire wedding invitation, that’ll be clearer.”
Both burst into laughter, though Thino’s eyes kept returning to the message. She typed, deleted, retyped, and deleted again. Finally, her fingers settled on:
Good morning, Vishwa. Glad you reached safely. Take some rest!
She hovered over the send button, heart pounding. Why am I so nervous? It’s just a text... but to him, everything feels like a big deal.

At last, she pressed send. The three dots appeared—he was typing. Her whole morning had already been made, and every love song she heard that day seemed to be all about him.

The morning bell rang, and the classroom buzzed with chatter. Thino walked in with Kavya, still dazed from last night’s text, her lips refusing to stop smiling. Yazhini and Harini were already in their corner seats, waving enthusiastically.

"Oye! What's with that glowing face? Looks like someone got a marriage proposal," Yazhini teased.
Thino froze, clutching her books tighter. "Wh–what proposal? It's just... I used a new face wash," she stammered.
Kavya snorted so loudly that the whole row turned. "Face wash ah? Dei Yazhini, Harini... it's not face wash. It's Vishwa wash!"
Thino's jaw dropped. "Kavyaaa! Shut up!"
Harini leaned forward, wide-eyed. "Wait wait... Vishwa? As in... Vishwa, the club Chairman Vishwa?"
"Nooo way. Tell me you're joking!" Yazhini clapped her hands in shock.
Kavya smirked, sipping her juice box like she was narrating breaking news. "Joke ah? Yesterday night, Miss Meme Queen here was on call with Vishwa till... what, Thino? 3? 4? And when I was peacefully sleeping, she screamed and shook me awake because..." She paused dramatically. "... Vishwa texted her I love you."
Both Yazhini and Harini gasped so loudly that even the lecturer at the door looked their way before walking on.
"WHATTTT! Vishwa confessed? And you didn't tell us? You fraud!" Harini grabbed Thino's arm.
Yazhini pretended to faint. "Omg, our Thino... the secret meme admin... bagging the most wanted senior of the campus. This is HISTORY!"
Thino buried her face in her notebook. "It's not like that... he just... maybe... typed by mistake..."
"Oh please. Nobody accidentally types I love you. It's not like typing ilaneer instead of idly," Kavya rolled her eyes.
The whole gang burst out laughing.

"So, when's the engagement? Should I book the canteen for reception?" Yazhini teased.

"Or shall we make a new meme page—The Girl Who Got the Club chairman?" Harini giggled.

"I hate all of you," Thino groaned, hiding her red face. But her shy smile betrayed her.

The bell rang again, class settling, but the whispers didn't stop. From the back, Yazhini scribbled on a piece of paper and slid it to Thino. It read: Mrs. Thino Vishwa.

Thino nearly kicked her under the bench, while the other three tried not to burst into laughter.

And just like that, the gang of four had a brand-new secret to giggle over between lectures, teases that wouldn't let Thino live in peace. It had only been three days, but Thino felt like she had lived a century of fulfillment. Her thoughts were consumed entirely by him—by Vishwa, and the sound of his voice that lingered in every corner of her mind.

The lecturer droned on about some boring circuit diagram while Thino's phone buzzed quietly under the desk. She sneakily checked it—Vishwa: "Had lunch?" Her fingers flew across the screen, her face glowing like the phone itself was radiating happiness. Kavya leaned over, whispering with a grin, "Look at her fingers flying. For assignments, she types one line per day, but for Vishwa, full essay!" Yazhini smirked, adding, "If sir asks her the diagram, she'll probably answer: 'Sorry sir, I'm in love.'" Harini covered her mouth, giggling, "See her smile... like she's watching Vijay Sethupathi movie climax." Suddenly, the lecturer's voice cut through her daydream: "Thino, what's the answer?" Startled, Thino blurted out without thinking, "I love you—uhh... I mean... voltage divider rule!"

The whole class erupted into laughter as she sank into her seat, glaring at her friends.
During the canteen break, the gang sat with plates of samosas, but Thino barely touched hers, her thumbs dancing on the phone screen. Vishwa's text popped up: "Don't skip snacks. You always forget." She giggled, replying, "How do you even know? Are you secretly spying on me?" Kavya snatched her plate. "Aiyo, why waste food? She's already full after eating Vishwa's words." Yazhini added, "Correct. For her, the menu is simple: breakfast—Vishwa, lunch—Vishwa, dinner—Vishwa." Harini sighed dramatically, "True love, da. Even oil samosa looks like rose petals when Vishwa texts." Thino blushed, shoving a samosa in her mouth just to quiet them.

After college, the four walked back to their rented room, Thino glued to her phone again, texting with full focus. "Careful on road," Vishwa messaged. She smiled, typing back, "Don't worry, I'm fine." She nearly collided with a cyclist, but Kavya pulled her back just in time. "See? Even Google Maps can't distract people this much!" Yazhini teased. "If one day she falls into a pothole, I swear the first text she'll send is: 'Vishwa, I fell down.' Not even 108 ambulance!" Everyone laughed, but Thino pretended not to hear.

That night in the hostel, the three girls were ready to sleep, the lights dimmed. Thino, however, stayed under her blanket, her face glowing from the phone. Vishwa's message popped up: "Did you smile today?" She typed, "Only now." "Then my day's complete," he replied.

She melted on the spot. Kavya peeked from her bed. "Dei! At this point, even mosquitoes in our room are jealous of you." Harini groaned, "I want to sleep, but her giggles sound like kutty love songs." Yazhini, with a sly grin, suggested, "Shall we tell Vishwa directly to reduce his romantic words after 11 pm? Because we need sleep!" Thino buried her face in the pillow, still smiling like an idiot.

The next day in the library, the usual silence prevailed until Thino's phone buzzed with a "ting ting" notification. In her hurry to reply, she forgot to mute her keyboard. The loud tik tik tik echoed across the quiet room, drawing the librarian's glare. "Silence, please!" Kavya whispered, struggling to contain laughter, "Shhh... not library. It's Love-brary now." Thino turned pink, hiding her phone behind her notes, while the girls tried not to giggle.

After classes, Kavya left for her hometown for the holidays. Thino waved at her, "Take care d.." Kavya smiled, "I know, you take care of you first... will be back tomorrow." Thino replied, "Bye byeeeee...", clutching her phone a little tighter, her thoughts drifting back to Vishwa once again.

The Silence Between the Lines

chapter 20
The Silence Between the Lines

Days rolled by, but something had started to shift. At first, everything felt the same—morning wishes, random jokes, late-night talks—but slowly, Thino noticed tiny cracks in the pattern she had once cherished. His cheerful "Good morning" became a curt "gm." His long, heartfelt replies dwindled into single words. Calls reduced, and sometimes he wouldn't pick up at all, sending a brief "Busy. Sorry." later. Thino tried to brush it off, convincing herself it was stress, college deadlines, or something else—but deep inside, her heart knew it wasn't the same.

That night, unable to sleep with the unease gnawing at her, she finally texted him: "Vishwa, what's wrong? You're not talking like before... did I do something?" Minutes passed. The typing dots appeared, disappeared, then appeared again. Finally, a message came: "Nothing... don't overthink." But that only made her overthink more, twisting her stomach with anxiety.

Unable to bear the silence, Thino called him. After a long pause, his voice finally came through the line, softer than usual. "Vishwa... please tell me the truth. You're not you these days," she pleaded. The line was silent; she could hear him breathing heavily. Then, breaking finally, he whispered, "Thino... I don't know how to say this... I think... I rushed into all this."

Thino froze, her chest tightening. “What do you mean?” she asked, voice trembling. “I... I still have a part of me that belongs to the girl I loved before. That letter I wrote... I didn’t think, I just confessed in the heat of the moment. I wanted to move on... but I’m not sure I really have,” he admitted. Every word cut into her chest like a knife. “So... all this time... was I just... a distraction?” she whispered, barely audible.

There was a pause, silence stretching longer than any explanation. “No... you mean a lot to me, Thino. But... I’m broken. I thought I was ready. Maybe I was wrong,” he finally said. Her fingers trembled as they gripped the phone. She didn’t cry—not yet—but felt numb, like a stone sinking in a cold river. “I never expected this from you, Vishwa. Not this low...” she said, her voice cold, and hung up.

Alone in her room, she sat staring at the blank wall, disconnected from the laughter of her friends echoing somewhere in the hostel corridor. Her phone buzzed—a message from him: “I’m sorry. I never wanted to hurt you.” She didn’t reply. For the first time in days, her screen remained dark. Inside her chest, a storm raged—anger, disbelief, sorrow, and the deep ache of someone who had just tasted love, only to have it snatched away.

The following morning, Thino woke with a heavy chest, her mind still tangled in the events of the previous night. Sleep had been a stranger, and the glow of her phone screen was the only company she had in the dark hours. By dawn, the numbness that had settled over her heart had slowly morphed into simmering anger.

She tapped out a message, erased it, rewrote, deleted again, and finally pressed send: "Vishwa, if you were unsure, why did you pull me into this? Why give me hope only to leave it dangling?" Minutes felt like hours before a reply blinked onto her screen. "I thought I knew what I felt. I really did, in that moment. But the truth is... I'm not whole yet. I'm still tangled in my past," he wrote. Her chest tightened. The words that were supposed to explain only deepened the storm within her. The call button was pressed almost instinctively. When he picked up, there was a pause, heavy and suffocating. His voice was quiet, hesitant, almost pleading: "Thino..." She cut him off, trembling, teeth clenched: "Don't. Don't even start with my name. Just tell me—why did you do it?" Her fingers dug into the bedsheet as if she could anchor herself against the whirlwind of her emotions. Her heart ached with betrayal, yet a part of her longed for him to interrupt with some miraculous explanation, a line that could make her whole again. But he stayed silent too long, and the stillness made her ache deeper.

"I wasn't lying," he finally said, voice shaky, a mixture of guilt and frustration threading through every syllable. "Then why, Vishwa? Was it a game? Was it a momentary thrill?" Her voice rose, cracking with anguish. "It was real... I meant every word when I said it," he shot back, almost defensive, yet she could hear the uncertainty underlying it. His words stumbled out, fragile and incomplete, as if he were trying to catch the truth before it fell apart in his own hands. "In that moment? So love is just a fleeting feeling to you?" Her laughter was hollow, bitter. Her chest tightened as tears pricked her eyes, a mixture of hurt and longing.

Her voice rose, cracking with anguish. "It was real... I meant every word when I said it," he shot back, almost defensive, yet she could hear the uncertainty underlying it. His words stumbled out, fragile and incomplete, as if he were trying to catch the truth before it fell apart in his own hands. "In that moment? So love is just a fleeting feeling to you?" Her laughter was hollow, bitter. Her chest tightened as tears pricked her eyes, a mixture of hurt and longing.

He tried to explain, but she would not listen calmly. "Don't twist it! I meant it then! I meant it!" he insisted. She felt the weight of every syllable pressing down on her chest, and every memory of laughter, every late-night conversation, every whispered care now felt like shards of glass slicing through her. "Then tell me, Vishwa. Tell me what I was to you. A distraction? A remedy for your loneliness?" she whispered, the bitterness in her voice masking the trembling vulnerability beneath.

"No, that's not it," he said, voice cracking. "I wasn't trying to hurt you... I thought I could move on, I thought I could feel again. You... you brought life back to me, just for a little while." Each word felt like a knife twisting inside her chest. "So all I ever was to you... was temporary relief? A patch for your wounds?" she asked, voice icy yet fragile. He didn't respond immediately, and the silence itself was louder than any denial he could have offered.

"I don't even know what I feel anymore. I'm broken, Thino. I'm trying to make sense, but everything is messy inside," he confessed, desperation creeping into his voice. Her tears came freely now, yet she held herself with rigid composure. "And you broke me while trying to fix yourself," she cried, feeling her world tilt into fragments. Her trust, given so freely, had been handled carelessly, and the realization made her hollow inside. "I can't... I won't love someone who treats me like a temporary cure," she whispered, voice shaking, yet firm in its finality.

The conversation ended, leaving behind a chasm neither could cross. Thino stared at the blank wall of her room, letting the silence engulf her. Her pillow was wet with silent tears, her chest tight with grief and lingering disbelief. She refused to text again, refusing to be the one to reach out, clinging instead to the bitter clarity that he had chosen his unresolved past over her. Across the city, Vishwa lay in his own room, staring at her contact, his hands trembling, guilt gnawing at him for the irrevocable damage done. What had begun with laughter, sweet words, and dreams spun together under late-night lights ended in a void of unspoken words, regret, and hearts too full to bear the weight of the truth. Both were left in fragments—not because they didn't care, but because their care had collided with timing, fear, and the unhealed corners of a past neither could ignore.

X

When Words Become Knives

chapter 21
When Words Become Knives

He tried to explain, but she would not listen calmly. "Don't twist it! I meant it then! I meant it!" he insisted. She felt the weight of every syllable pressing down on her chest, and every memory of laughter, every late-night conversation, every whispered care now felt like shards of glass slicing through her. "Then tell me, Vishwa. Tell me what I was to you. A distraction? A remedy for your loneliness?" she whispered, the bitterness in her voice masking the trembling vulnerability beneath.

"No, that's not it," he said, voice cracking. "I wasn't trying to hurt you... I thought I could move on, I thought I could feel again. You... you brought life back to me, just for a little while." Each word felt like a knife twisting inside her chest. "So all I ever was to you... was temporary relief? A patch for your wounds?" she asked, voice icy yet fragile. He didn't respond immediately, and the silence itself was louder than any denial he could have offered.

"I don't even know what I feel anymore. I'm broken, Thino. I'm trying to make sense, but everything is messy inside," he confessed, desperation creeping into his voice. Her tears came freely now, yet she held herself with rigid composure. "And you broke me while trying to fix yourself," she cried, feeling her world tilt into fragments. Her trust, given so freely, had been handled carelessly, and the realization made her hollow inside. "I can't... I won't love someone who treats me like a temporary cure," she whispered, voice shaking, yet firm in its finality.

The conversation ended, leaving behind a chasm neither could cross. Thino stared at the blank wall of her room, letting the silence engulf her. Her pillow was wet with silent tears, her chest tight with grief and lingering disbelief. She refused to text again, refusing to be the one to reach out, clinging instead to the bitter clarity that he had chosen his unresolved past over her. Across the city, Vishwa lay in his own room, staring at her contact, his hands trembling, guilt gnawing at him for the irrevocable damage done. What had begun with laughter, sweet words, and dreams spun together under late-night lights ended in a void of unspoken words, regret, and hearts too full to bear the weight of the truth. Both were left in fragments—not because they didn't care, but because their care had collided with timing, fear, and the unhealed corners of a past neither could ignore.

Thino's Room

The call ended. The screen went dark, leaving Thino alone with her reflection on the black glass. Her eyes were swollen, her hands trembling as she let the phone rest on the bed beside her. Her chest rose and fell in uneven gasps. The silence of her room felt like a crushing weight, pressing down on every corner of her heart.

It's really over... she thought, gripping the pillow tighter, pressing it against her chest as though it could hold together the fragments of her shattered heart. Every inhale burned; every exhale carried the weight of betrayal. She curled into herself, trying to hold in the tears, but they came anyway—soft at first, then in unstoppable streams.

Her mind played the conversation on repeat: his voice breaking, his words slicing through her: "You started everything. I didn't."

Thino whispered into the darkness, voice brittle: "Why did you say it, Vishwa? Why make me believe?" When she loved, it was with her whole being, unreserved, absolute. And she had loved him fully, every fleeting moment of it, without hesitation. How could he casually unravel it all with a single careless confession? A week for him, but a lifetime in her heart. She pressed the pillow harder, sobbing into it, imagining the life she had begun to weave around him—now scattered into nothing.

The night stretched endlessly. Her phone buzzed once—Kavya's message: "You okay?" Thino stared at it, her chest tightening further. She didn't respond. Words would have been meaningless. Eventually, exhaustion claimed her, dragging her into a restless sleep, body curled around the pillow as if it could fill the void Vishwa had left.

Vishwa's Room

Meanwhile, Vishwa sat on the edge of his bed, phone in hand, staring at her name in the call log. He could almost hear her voice if he concentrated, but the sound only made the ache worse. His room, normally cluttered with the careless chaos of a college life, went unnoticed. Inside, his mind was deafening.

What have I done? Why did I say those words? Why couldn't I just be honest? he thought, burying his face in his hands.

His chest tightened painfully. He wanted to call back, a hundred times over, but every attempt stopped short.

She deserves better... someone certain, not someone fractured and lost like me.

Guilt clawed at him relentlessly. Every laugh, every meme she sent, every casual goodnight—it all stabbed now. He tossed the phone onto the bed and buried his face in his palms, letting out a scream that remained trapped in his chest, invisible but scorching. Sleep eventually pulled him down, restless and heavy, while the thought of her enduring this pain haunted him.

The Silence Between Them.

Two hearts that had once roared with laughter and warmth now lay fractured, miles apart. Both ached, both missed the other, yet the wall of unspoken words and misaligned timing grew higher with each passing moment. That night, no one moved. No one spoke.

Morning, College

Kavya returned to the hostel and immediately sensed something was wrong. Thino, usually lively, sarcastic, and inseparable from her phone, was a shadow. In class, she sat still, scribbling nothing, her eyes swollen and dull.

“Hey... you okay?” Kavya asked softly, leaning closer.

Thino forced a faint smile. “Yeah... just... didn’t sleep well.”

“Thino, don’t lie. Your face tells the story your words won’t,” Kavya said gently.

Thino turned away, cold. “I said I’m fine.” Something in her eyes—heavier, darker—made Kavya stop pressing.

Night, Balcony

The night air was cool, but it didn't reach her. Thino sat on the balcony floor, phone dark in her hand, no new messages. Inside, Kavya paced, noting every silence, every untouched plate, every unspoken word.

When Thino left her phone momentarily, Kavya hesitated before picking it up. Unlocking it, her heart sank. The last messages from Vishwa blinked back:

"I still have a part for the girl I loved..."

"I confessed without thinking... I'm sorry, Thino."

Kavya's stomach twisted as the pieces clicked into place.

She found Thino on the stairs, knees hugged to her chest, head bowed. Shadows cast by the dim light above made her look fragile, almost unreal. Kavya sat beside her silently, wrapping her arms around Thino.

"Don't... don't worry, Thino. Everything will be okay... I promise," she whispered.

The moment those words reached her, Thino broke completely. Her body shook, sobs ripping through her as she buried her face in Kavya's shoulder.

"No, Kavya! It won't be okay! It won't!" she cried.

Kavya tightened her hold. "Shhh... Thino..."

"I loved him... with everything I had. Every day, every thought, every dream... and he just—" Her voice cracked. "—he just threw me away like I meant nothing!"

Kavya's own throat tightened at the rawness. "Thino... I had no idea it was this deep..."

"You don't understand! He was my world! Every plan, every little thing reminded me of him! And now... he calls it a mistake? Who does that? Who plays with someone's heart like that?!"
Kavya stroked her hair, whispering, "He's a fool... a complete fool to hurt you. You gave him your whole heart."
Thino leaned back slightly, soaked in tears, whispering brokenly, "The worst part... the worst part is he made me believe. He made me feel loved. And I clung to it... like it was everything."

Kavya's chest ached alongside hers. "If I could take this pain away, I would, Thino. I swear I would."
Thino let out a shuddering breath. "I wanted to believe... that not everyone leaves. That love could be real for me. But he... he proved that even when it seems certain, it can break you."

Kavya held her tighter, murmuring over and over, "It's going to be alright. I'm here. You're not alone."
For the first time, Kavya truly understood the depth of Thino's love for Vishwa. This wasn't a fleeting crush or teenage infatuation—it was a piece of her soul poured out completely. And seeing her shatter, Kavya felt her own heart fracture in sympathy, holding her friend through the endless storm of grief and betrayal.

Nights That Never End

chapter 22
Nights That Never End

Every night was the same. When the hostel lights dimmed, when laughter and chatter finally faded from the corridors, silence found Thino—and in that silence, her grief began again. Kavya had thought, perhaps, that it would pass after the first night. Tears, she believed, were like storms—loud, heavy, but fleeting. But she was wrong. Each night, like clockwork, Thino broke all over again. The muffled sobs, the sharp breaths, the sound of a pillow being crushed too tightly—these became the soundtrack of her nights.

On the first night, Kavya lay on her side pretending to sleep, but Thino's whisper cut through the darkness like a knife. "Why... why would he say those words if he didn't mean them? Does he even know I'm breaking every second? Does he know I can't breathe without thinking of him?" Her voice cracked under the weight of her confession, followed by sobs that seemed too big for her small frame. Kavya bit her lip, fighting her own tears. She wanted to hold her, but Thino had turned to the wall, curled in on herself as if she wanted to disappear.

By the third night, Kavya woke to find Thino sitting by the balcony door, knees pulled up, her swollen eyes staring blankly into the dark. "Thino... come lie down, please. You'll fall sick," Kavya whispered gently.

But Thino didn't move. Her voice came out hollow, stripped of life: "Do you know what hurts the most? Not that he left me... but that I still want him. I still want the very person who broke me. I can't even hate him. I just..." Her words dissolved into silence, but her trembling shoulders spoke what her lips could not. Kavya had no answer.

On the sixth night, it was past midnight when Thino clutched her phone tightly to her chest, tears streaming down her cheeks. "Why hasn't he even messaged once? Was I really that easy to erase? Was I just a mistake?" she whispered between sobs. "I gave him everything... every laugh, every secret, every piece of me. And now I feel empty, Kavya. Empty..." Kavya sat beside her, stroking her hair, wishing she could say something that would take the pain away. She wanted to tell her, You still have me, but she knew those words would never fill the hollow Vishwa had left behind.

By the tenth night, Kavya's heart had begun breaking in a different way. She wasn't just witnessing heartbreak; she was watching her best friend slowly unravel, piece by fragile piece. Thino barely ate, her laughter had become a memory, and her silence screamed louder than her tears. That night, she shattered harder than before, burying her face in her pillow as her voice broke into a scream. "I hate him! I hate him for making me love him this much! I hate him for ruining me like this! Why wasn't I enough, Kavya? Tell me! Why wasn't I enough?

What did she have that I didn't?" Kavya's tears spilled freely as she held Thino's fists gently, as if she were calming a child. "Shhh... please, don't hurt yourself. Please, Thino... you are enough. You always were. You loved more than anyone else could." But Thino only shook her head violently. "Then why am I here crying alone every night? Why does he get to walk away while I drown in this pain?" The question echoed through the dark with no answer.
Kavya lay awake long after Thino cried herself into exhaustion. She stared at the ceiling, whispering silent prayers in her heart. Please let her survive this. Please don't let this pain kill her spirit. But the nights kept coming. And so did the tears. Days followed the same cruel rhythm. Slowly, Thino withdrew into a haunting quietness. Sometimes she would sit in one place for hours, like a statue carved from grief, and Kavya stayed with her through every collapse and consequence.

Each morning arrived too soon. With swollen eyes and a pale face, Thino would drag herself out of bed, force a smile in the mirror, and prepare to face the world. In class, she laughed at jokes, teased back when poked, even joined conversations—but her laugh was no longer hers. It was measured, practiced, a shield rather than an expression. To everyone else, she looked fine. But Kavya could see the emptiness behind the mask.

On their walks back to the hostel, Thino often lagged a little behind, her eyes catching on the couples around campus—walking hand in hand, whispering, laughing.

Her lips curled into a faint smile, but her eyes glistened with unshed tears. “They don’t even know how lucky they are… to be wanted, to be chosen,” she whispered under her breath. Kavya slowed her steps to match hers. “Stop doing that,” she said softly. Thino blinked. “Doing what?” “Smiling while you’re bleeding inside,” Kavya replied gently. Thino’s lips trembled, but she said nothing, only clutching her bag tighter to her chest.

When they reached the room, Kavya made a decision. She grabbed a notebook and pen, placed them firmly in Thino’s trembling hands, and said, “Here. Write. Write every word, every scream, every memory. Curse him if you want. Pour it all out here instead of pouring it into yourself. Promise me, Thino. Promise me you won’t keep this poison locked inside.”

Thino stared at the notebook, tears falling onto the blank page. “What if… what if writing it makes it real?” she whispered. Kavya’s voice grew fierce despite the softness in her tone. “It is real, Thino. Keeping it inside won’t erase it. But letting it out—that’s the only way you’ll ever breathe again.”

Finally, with shaking hands, Thino pressed the pen to the page. Her writing was jagged, messy, raw—but with every line, something released. Every stroke of the pen was a sob leaving her chest, every word a piece of pain she no longer carried alone.

Kavya sat beside her, one arm wrapped tightly around her shoulders, silent but unyielding in her support. And for the first time in days, Thino's grief was no longer swallowed by the night. It had a place to live, outside her heart, written into existence.

From Tears to Words, From Words to a Voice

chapter 23

From Tears to Words, From Words to a Voice

very night, the balcony light stood as Thino's only witness, its pale glow spilling across her trembling hands as she poured herself into the blank notebook that no longer stayed blank for long. At first, the pages carried nothing but broken words, scattered confessions of a heart too raw to hide its pain – "I miss you." "Why wasn't I enough?" "Why did you stay just to leave?" But slowly, those jagged words began to shift, transforming into lines of reflection, of anger, of humor so dark it almost startled her. The ink no longer only bled; it burned. One night, when Kavya quietly stepped onto the balcony and caught a glimpse of the notebook, she froze. It wasn't pain anymore – it was something else, something alive, a voice carved out of heartbreak. "Thino... this isn't just crying on paper," she whispered in awe, "this is you." Thino, startled and ashamed, wiped her tears quickly, insisting they were just meaningless scribbles no one would ever want to read. But Kavya's eyes blazed with conviction as she shook her head. "No, these words hit like arrows. They're raw, real. People need to feel this. You always had a voice – and now you've found it." She placed her phone in Thino's trembling hands, urging her to share, to turn the notebook's silent screams into something louder.

Thino's fear was evident as she whispered, "What if they laugh? What if they don't understand?" But Kavya only smiled, steady and certain, holding her hand as if anchoring her. "Then let them laugh. Let them not understand. At least you'll breathe. This page isn't just memes anymore, Thino – it's your battlefield, your diary in disguise." With a shaky breath, Thino typed her first raw caption, a truth dressed in irony: "Funny thing about heartbreak? The person who made you believe in forever is also the one teaching you endings are real." She paired it with a biting meme, half dark, half mocking of her own wound, and pressed post. Her heart thundered, her chest tightened and lifted at once, and within minutes her phone lit up with a flood of responses – likes, comments, shares. Some laughed. Some connected. Some whispered, "This is exactly what I needed today." For the first time in weeks, Thino felt something stir back to life inside her, a spark where there had only been ash. Kavya, sitting beside her, watched the glow of the screen reflect in her eyes and grinned. "See? I told you. Your pain just turned into power. Your silence just became a voice." Thino exhaled, her lips trembling into a fragile but real smile, tears glistening as she whispered back, "Maybe... maybe this is how I heal. Not by forgetting him, but by remembering myself."

The next afternoon, the canteen buzzed with laughter and chatter, but at a corner table three friends sat weighed down by worry. Thino's chair was empty; instead, she lay curled in her hostel bed, curtains drawn tight, too drained to face the world. Harini and Yazhini, restless with unease, had pulled Kavya aside, their voices low but heavy with frustration. "Dei Kavya... what's happening to her?" Yazhini asked, her brows furrowed. "It's been days. She's not coming out, not laughing, not even smiling. This is not the Thino I know." Harini leaned forward with a sigh, her tone tinged with disbelief. "Exactly. Just a few weeks of love, right? They hardly even knew each other properly. Why is she so shattered like this? People break up all the time and move on. Why can't she?" Kavya sat silently for a long moment, lips pressed into a thin line as she set her coffee cup down. When she finally spoke, her words were slow but sharp with conviction. "You both don't understand. To you it may look like 'few weeks of love,' but for her... it was not weeks. It was everything. She didn't just like him because of excitement or attention. She gave him her trust—and Thino is not the kind of girl who gives that easily." Yazhini shook her head, still puzzled. "But Kavya... how deep can it get in such a short time? She's strong. I've seen her face failures, rejections, even insults without breaking down. But this? She's crying every night. I mean... is he really worth all this?"

Kavya's eyes hardened as she leaned in closer, her voice trembling with a protective edge. "Worth it or not doesn't matter. You don't see what I see every night. She loved him without asking anything in return. She never demanded, never questioned, never forced. She just believed in his words, held onto them like her life depended on it. That's who she is. When Thino loves, she doesn't do it half-heartedly—she pours all of herself into it."

Harini's voice softened, but her doubt lingered. "But still, Kavya... he broke it in days. Shouldn't she just let go instead of holding this pain?" At that, Kavya's composure cracked, her voice unsteady as tears threatened. "Do you even hear yourself? Let go? If it were you—if the person you trusted with all your heart suddenly told you it meant nothing—could you just smile and move on the next day? Do you know what it's like to see her sit on the stairs at night, hugging her knees, shaking, crying so silently that sometimes I wonder if she'll stop breathing? Do you know how it feels when I hug her and she collapses in my arms like a child, whispering, 'why me, Kavya?'" Her words fell heavy, leaving Harini and Yazhini stunned into silence, guilt flickering across their faces.

Kavya wiped at her own damp eyes, her tone softening as she continued. "She's not crying because she lost a boy. She's crying because she lost her faith. She trusted him blindly, believed every word, and when that broke... it shattered something inside her.

You see her as bold, fun-loving Thino. But I see the girl who whispers to herself before sleeping, 'I just wanted him to be real.'" Yazhini bit her lip, eyes brimming, while Harini exhaled deeply, her earlier frustration melting into sorrow. "I didn't know it was this bad," she admitted quietly. "I thought it was just... a fling." Kavya shook her head firmly. "No. Thino is not the for-show type. If she loves, she loves like she's placing her soul in someone else's hands. That's why it hurts this much. You can't measure her love by days or weeks—you measure it by the way she's breaking now. If you saw her pain even once, you'd never say she should just move on." The three of them sat in silence then, the noise of the canteen suddenly feeling distant and hollow. Harini and Yazhini exchanged a glance, guilt etched into their faces, before Yazhini whispered softly, "Dei Kavya... we didn't realize. We'll be careful with her. We won't tease or push. We'll just... be there." Kavya nodded, her eyes heavy with unshed tears, but her voice steady as she replied, "That's all I ask. She doesn't need lectures. She doesn't need advice. She just needs us to sit beside her—until she remembers how to smile again."

Weeks slipped by, and though Thino no longer cried herself to sleep every night, it wasn't healing that stopped her tears—it was exhaustion. With Kavya faithfully at her side, acting as her shadow, Thino had simply learned to bury the ache deeper, wrapping it in layers of busyness that fooled everyone except those who truly knew her.

In college, she became the girl who was always occupied: sketching storyboards in the cultural club office, staying late in the media room editing short films, filling the margins of her notebooks with half-scribbled poems that no one else was meant to read. To the outside world, she was "fine"—active, reliable, even admirable. But to her close friends, she wasn't the same. Something about her had gone missing.

Inside the cultural club office, a group of students huddled around a whiteboard as Thino's marker scratched across it, her voice calm and steady. "So, the last scene has to end with silence... because silence sometimes speaks louder than words. Got it?" she explained, and the juniors nodded, wide-eyed, whispering to each other how cool she was, how her ideas always carried weight.

But from the back of the room, Kavya watched with a knowing heaviness in her chest. She could hear what the others couldn't—the absence of mischief in Thino's tone, the way her laughter had been replaced by a quiet discipline. This wasn't passion alone; it was distraction, a desperate effort to keep herself too occupied to think.

Late at night, when the campus had quieted, the truth surfaced in her notebook. Thino sat at her desk, a crumpled page beneath her trembling hand, messy words scrawled in the dim light. "You lit a fire in me, and then left me burning alone. I smile in the daylight, but at night, my ashes write these words."

She stared at the lines, her eyes blurred, whispering into the empty room, "Why do I still write about you? Why do I still... feel you here?" Kavya entered quietly, draping a blanket over her shoulders, her voice soft yet steady. "Because love like yours doesn't disappear in a few weeks. It lingers. It hurts. But it also means you were real." Thino blinked back her tears, closing the notebook quickly, masking her heart with a forced smile. "I'm fine, Kavya. See? I'm writing, I'm working, I'm... busy." Kavya didn't argue; she only wrapped her arms around her from behind, knowing that "fine" was the biggest lie Thino told herself.

In the canteen one afternoon, Harini nudged her playfully. "Hey, why so serious? You used to roast us daily, remember? Tease Yazhini until she cried?" Yazhini laughed in agreement, "Yeah! You haven't bullied me in weeks. What happened to the old Thino?" Thino gave them both a small, polite smile, but her silence lingered longer than her smile. She only sipped her juice quietly, and Kavya quickly shifted the conversation before the others could press further. Later, when the group had dispersed, Kavya leaned closer, her tone gentle but firm. "You're still here, da. But your spark... it's hiding." Thino said nothing, just rested her head on the table, staring blankly at the tiled floor.

Her silence spoke louder than any words could. And when she walked alone across campus at dusk, the emptiness echoed even louder.

Her thoughts spilled restlessly inside her: "I'm doing everything right. Clubs, projects, poetry... I'm living. Then why does it still feel like half of me is missing? Why do I still wake up hoping for a message that never comes? Why... can't I be the girl I used to be?" Her eyes watered, but she quickly brushed the tears away before anyone could notice. She pulled out her phone, scrolled through old photos, then locked the screen as though punishing herself for even looking. She exhaled sharply, forcing her steps forward.

On the surface, she looked as though she was thriving—creative, hardworking, respected. But her closest ones saw the cracks. She was living, yes... but not laughing. Working, yes... but not playing. She was still loving, though only through the wounds that love had left behind. Her nights bled poetry, her days hid behind silence. She was surviving... but far from healed.

Her Real Voice of Sadness

chapter 24
Her Real Voice of Sadness

The third year began with its usual rush of projects, events, and club work, and Thino threw herself into everything she could—media editing, cultural activities, short films, scribbling poetry—anything that kept her busy and distracted from the ache in her chest. Outwardly, she seemed fine, but those who knew her well, especially Kavya, noticed how her laughter no longer carried the same playful spark, how her teasing had dulled into silence, and how her mischievous glow seemed buried beneath her exhaustion. Hoping to ease her heaviness, the girls—Thino, Kavya, Harini, and Yazhini—planned a short trip to Pondicherry, believing a change of scenery might help her breathe again. Inside a pub one night, surrounded by loud music and flashing lights, their corner table felt quieter, like a small bubble away from the chaos, and after a few drinks Thino's carefully constructed mask began to slip. Yazhini leaned closer, remarking that it felt good to see her smile after so many months, but Thino laughed bitterly and confessed that it wasn't a real smile, only a performance for her friends, because the truth was far more painful.

Harini encouraged her to share what she kept locked away, and slowly Thino admitted that every time she laughed, she heard Vishwa's name in her head, and every time she wrote, her words became his reflection, until she realized that no matter how much she filled her life with clubs and projects, she had built a stage where only he still stood.

Kavya reached out and gently told her that she had loved deeply and didn't need to erase that so quickly, but Thino shook her head and said there was no point, because he wasn't there, he hadn't chosen her, and if she confessed her pain openly, people would only tell her to move on, as if it were as simple as throwing away an old notebook. Her voice cracked as she continued, saying she hated him for leaving her with silence, hated herself even more for still wishing he would call her name, and she cried openly, calling herself stupid for waiting for someone who made it clear he didn't want her. The table fell into a heavy silence, but Kavya quickly pulled her into a hug, wiping her tears and telling her she had said enough, though Thino insisted on adding that despite everything, she still remembered the boy who had once spoken to her with kindness and care, and that was the version she couldn't forget. Later, back at the hotel while the others slept, Thino lay restless, her heart weighed down by everything she had confessed, until in a blur she picked up her phone and dialed Vishwa's number.

To her shock, he answered, groggy from sleep, and she began to pour out her truth, telling him she had tried everything to forget him but always circled back, that she hated it but missed him like hell, and when he asked why she was saying all this now, she laughed weakly through her tears and admitted that she was simply too tired to lie to herself anymore. Before she could finish her words, sleep pulled her under mid-sentence, and Vishwa sat awake on the other end, clutching his phone as her breathing echoed softly through the line.

The next morning, Thino woke in the hotel room with a pounding head and no memory of the night before, only to be met with the mischievous grins of Kavya, Harini, and Yazhini, who teased her relentlessly, claiming she had become a drunk poet, philosopher, and even a late-night radio jockey, confessing her feelings about Vishwa openly. Horrified, Thino buried her face in a pillow as they recited her supposed drunken words, laughing that she had sung heartbreak songs and even called him "my sunshine" over the phone. Mortified beyond belief, she groaned and begged them to stop, only to have them continue teasing her all the way through the trip, at the beach, and even on the bus ride back to college, with Harini parodying love songs, Yazhini dramatizing her late-night confessions, and Kavya reminding her that while she remembered nothing, Vishwa had heard everything. Thino kept groaning, hiding her face in embarrassment, muttering that she was officially dead and questioning why she was even friends with them, but deep inside her heart beat faster, because beneath all the laughter and humiliation, the truth haunted her—Vishwa had heard every word, every tear, every laugh, and for the first time in years, she had been completely, painfully honest.

The Convocation Encounter

chapter 25
The Convocation Encounter

The convocation day finally arrived after weeks of rehearsals and preparation. The grand auditorium was filled with restless energy, the kind that only came on such days. Proud parents sat with phones and cameras ready, professors whispered among themselves, and students in their robes laughed and posed for photos, the atmosphere buzzing with anticipation. At the very back of the hall, away from the center of the excitement, Thino adjusted the live camera feed, her headphones resting over her ears, eyes fixed on the monitor. Beside her, Kavya was checking the microphones and making sure the live-stream connection didn't falter. Only she knew the truth—this was Vishwa's batch. For days, she had carried the secret like a weight, terrified of what it would do to Thino if she found out too soon. She didn't want to reopen the wounds that had barely scabbed over, didn't want to see her friend shatter again. In her heart, she repeated the same thought over and over: God, how do I even tell her? If she sees him... no, I can't. I'll protect her this time. I'll manage somehow.

But fate was crueler than intentions. When one of their friends called for Thino to check the side feed, she pulled down her headset and turned toward the door. And in that single moment, it happened. A glance—so brief it could be measured in less than a fraction of a second. Her eyes locked with Vishwa's across the crowd. The effect was violent, tearing through her chest with the sharpness of memory.

In that heartbeat, all the years of love, the ache of betrayal, and the silence that had drowned her rushed back, flooding her veins like fire. Vishwa froze too, his lips parting slightly, his expression shifting as if he had seen a ghost. His eyes softened instantly, betraying the storm inside him, a storm he hadn't expected. Thino, however, turned her face away almost instinctively, forcing her feet to keep moving. She walked past him as though he were just another graduate, her heart screaming in chaos while her body refused to stop.

Minutes passed and Thino did not return to her station. Kavya, sensing something was wrong, excused herself and searched the hall. She found Thino outside in the far corner of the building, crouched against the wall, her hands trembling uncontrollably.

"Thino... hey, breathe... just breathe..." Kavya whispered gently, kneeling beside her. Thino pressed her hand against her chest, her breathing shallow, her eyes wet with unshed tears. "Why... why did he have to come here today? After all this time..." she whispered, her voice breaking. Kavya's throat tightened with guilt. She had known. She had hidden it. And now the secret felt poisonous. "I'm sorry," she confessed, her voice cracking, "I should've told you earlier. I knew it was his batch... but I didn't want you to break before the program even started. I thought maybe you wouldn't meet him at all. I was scared to say it." The pain on Thino's face was the same one Kavya had seen two years ago—the same shattered expression, the same suffocating breathlessness.

It was true what people said: first love could never be erased so easily. It became a thorn inside the heart, tearing quietly until the end.

Yet, after a moment, Thino shut her eyes and inhaled deeply. When she opened them again, there was a quiet strength there. She wiped her tears roughly with the back of her hand and stood up. “No,” she said softly but firmly, “I’m not that girl anymore. I can’t run. Not today.” She squeezed Kavya’s hand and walked back inside. For the rest of the ceremony, she buried herself in work—fixing angles, adjusting wires, checking lights. Her hands moved with mechanical precision, but her mind was a battlefield. She didn’t dare lift her eyes toward the graduates. Vishwa, seated in the front row, could not stop himself from stealing glances. Every shadow that moved at the back of the hall made his heart stumble, every glimpse of her silhouette felt like a reminder of everything he had lost.

When the ceremony ended, chaos took over again. Families crowded around, hugging, laughing, clicking endless pictures. Thino quietly began gathering equipment, coiling wires with deliberate care, her movements slow and steady. And then she sensed it. Vishwa was walking toward her. For the first time in years, he was close enough to speak, close enough that she could hear his breath if she chose to listen. His lips parted, his voice trembling at the edge. “Thino—” he began. But before the moment could bloom, Kavya stepped forward swiftly, her polite smile masking a shield of steel.

"Excuse me," she said firmly, "we need to clear this place. Please move outside." Vishwa froze, torn between her words and the silent presence of Thino who kept her head down, refusing to meet his gaze, her fingers tightening around the coiled wires as though holding herself together.

He lingered. The hall emptied one by one, families leaving, laughter fading. Yet Vishwa stayed, standing still, waiting. Minutes bled into hours. He waited for her to look up, just once. But she never did. She never even glanced his way, not by accident, not by mercy. At last, with his shoulders heavy and his hope thinning to nothing, he understood. With every step he took toward the door, it felt as though a door inside him closed forever.

From the corner, Kavya watched in silence, her chest constricted by guilt. She turned to Thino and whispered, "He... he wanted to talk. Maybe start again. But I stopped him..." Thino's eyes flickered, but her face remained unreadable. She only whispered, almost to herself, "Some doors... once closed, should never be opened again." Her hands continued packing as if unaffected, but the silence around her was bleeding. Vishwa had waited, had stood there watching her for hours with the hope of just one glance, but she had given him nothing. And when he finally lowered his head and walked out of the college gate, Thino saw him from afar yet didn't move. Her body stayed still while her heart clenched in a silent cry.

Kavya touched her shoulder softly. “Come on, let’s go home. You did well today,” she murmured. Thino forced a smile, though inside her heart whispered bitterly: He waited. He wanted to talk. But no... not again. Not after all this. And so, with the weight of unspoken words crushing them, Thino and Vishwa walked away in opposite directions—backs turned, hearts heavy, everything unsaid hanging in the space between them like unfinished music.

The Last Chapter, A Quiet Goodbye

chapter 26
The Last Chapter , A Quiet Goodbye

Kavya's words lingered in Thino's mind that evening: "I felt like Vishwa wanted to talk to you."

Hope was a strange thing—it was fragile, but it refused to die. Even after years, even after endless pain, it somehow clung to life. And so, against every promise she had ever made to herself, Thino found her fingers betraying her resolve as they dialed his number once more.

The call was brief. His voice was warm enough, polite even, but it carried none of the weight she had once longed to hear. They spoke like two acquaintances, strangers bound only by a thin thread of memory, not like two hearts that had once almost belonged to each other. When the line fell silent, something in her chest tightened. She hated herself for it, hated how her self-respect vanished the moment it came to him.

Later, unable to still the storm within, she sent a message: "Can we meet?"

The reply came like the sound of a door slamming shut. "No. For what?"

She stared at the screen for minutes that felt like hours, waiting for words that would never come. And in that single, sharp response, the truth became undeniable. The thread she had been clutching for two years had already been cut. She had been holding on to nothing but air. And thino told kavya that she called him with a loosened sad face and with in a fraction of second kavya just gave a force and weight to her hand and just slapped her.

The sound was sharp, startling in its suddenness. Thino just didn't say anything for a while and kavya stared a death stare and thino told ' yeah...yeah...i needed that.' she admitted softly.

Vishwa's world was different now. He had closed that chapter long ago. When her name had flashed on his screen, for a fleeting second he had wondered—was there something left? Was there anything still binding them? But the conversation felt distant, cautious. To him, she seemed like someone who had moved on. When her message came asking to meet, he chose to leave it unanswered in spirit. It was easier that way. Safer. Cleaner. He had already walked away once, and he was not ready to turn back.

But Thino's world stopped for a while.

That night, she lay awake in the dark, silence pressing against her ribs. She wanted to cry, but no tears came. Only the quiet acceptance that this was the end—the end of her long, stubborn hope, the end of waiting, the end of believing that one day things might fall into place. That heavy feeling in the chest, the one that whispers there's nothing more you can do, finally settled into her bones.

It hurt—not with the wild tearing agony of the past, but with a softer, exhausted ache. A kind of grief that didn't scream anymore, but whispered.

And in that whispering silence, Thino began to write.

"Some loves are not lost.
They just remain unfinished.
Not forgotten. Just carried.
Like a scar you no longer hide."

Time began to move again. Slowly at first, then faster, until days melted into months. Laughter returned to her lips—not the careless, playful laughter of the girl she once was, but something lighter, steadier. She still wrote poetry, still worked in clubs, still found small joys in life. She wasn't broken anymore, but she wasn't the same. She had grown into someone calmer, someone who knew how to carry love without letting it drown her.

Vishwa lived on somewhere else, untouched by her absence. Not everyone loved with words. Some loved with silence. Some with waiting. Some with pain. Thino had loved him in every way, and in doing so, she had unknowingly destroyed parts of herself. But now she was learning. Because moving on didn't mean erasing him—it meant carrying the memory with peace.

And so she closed that chapter of her heart—not with anger, not with regret, but with quiet love. The kind of love that stays even after it ends.

A year later, as she entered her final year, her club was preparing for its annual inauguration. The hall buzzed with soft chatter as students gathered, some curious, some excited. On the small stage, Thino stood with a book in her hands—her book. The cover was simple, her name printed in gentle letters at the bottom.

"This," she began softly, her voice trembling at first, "is not just a story. It's a part of me. A journey I never thought I would share."

Her friends, Kavya and the others, exchanged quiet glances. They had seen her smile when she was breaking, had watched her laugh when her heart was heavy. But none of them truly knew how much she had carried inside.

The audience leaned forward as she opened the first page.

The story she read was about a girl who once believed in a boy with all her heart. A girl who waited, who hoped, who held onto tiny sparks even after the fire had gone out. She read about drunken calls, teasing friends, trips filled with laughter where pain had hidden beneath the surface. She wrote of the night she finally reached out—only to realize he had already moved on.

Her words were tender, never bitter. She did not blame him. She did not curse fate. She only wrote the truth—raw, fragile, human.

And in the final chapter, she wrote:

“Sometimes love doesn’t stay. Sometimes it isn’t meant to. But that doesn’t make it less real. It doesn’t make it less beautiful. Some loves are carried, not lived. And this was mine. I moved on, yes. But I will always carry this love, quietly, like a bookmark in the story of my life.”

When she finished reading, the hall fell silent. Not applause, not immediately—just silence heavy with feeling. Then, slowly, hands began to clap. Soft at first, then louder, until the room was filled with the sound.

Kavya wiped her eyes, pride and sadness mixing in equal measure. Somewhere, perhaps in that crowd or perhaps far away,

Vishwa would never know the depth of the story written about him. But it no longer mattered. This was not his ending. It was hers.

From the audience, Yazhini frowned, her voice confused. "How could she even write about him after everything he did to her? After all that pain?"

Kavya laughed softly, remembering. "I asked her the same thing."

"And what was her reply?" Yazhini pressed.

Thino's lips curved into a light smile. "We're so distracted by how things end that we forget how beautiful the beginning was."

"Damn... this girl," Yazhini whispered, shaking her head, half in awe.

With that smile still lingering on her face, Thino closed the book. For the first time in years, she felt weightless. She had not only lived her story—she had written it, spoken it aloud, and finally let it go. Her love had not ended in silence or bitterness, but in words. Words that carried her pain, her hope, and her healing. A story that would live, even after she no longer needed it.

And so, she had nothing left to regret.

From the very last row, unnoticed by most, a boy sat quietly. He had listened to every word, every pause, every trembling breath. His lips curved into the faintest, most genuine smile as he whispered to himself, almost in awe:

"Do girls like her really exist?"

And just like that, what had once been an ending... also became a beginning.

THE END

LUKIEST UNLUCKY

How lucky she is ...

to have a Man who *loves* her like no other man can love

her like he do.

And how lucky *you are...*

to have one who love you like no other girl can love

like I do.

Yes , you both are lucky and the unluckiest is just me at

the

END.

ME? A POET ?

No... Absolutely *NOT*.

I don't write because I'm a Poet nor because

I want to be One .

I write from the wound - hurt,

struck by the arrow - people,

The unseen blood - ink;

The very Arrow , I weild as a pen.

And with every word , I write Myself whole and

HEAL.

EPILOGUE

They came to teach us that even heartbreak can be beautiful, that even distance leaves behind warmth, and that sometimes, letting go is another form of love. She was the one that got away twice, but she was also the one who stayed with herself, whole at last.

She improved her own worth and talents, proving that not everything that happens is meant to break you. What shatters and is reborn carries even greater value. If there is an end, there is always a new beginning and that's how it ends.

Author's Note

The One That Got Away Twice is not just about a character, but about anyone who has felt unseen yet found a way to speak and to express. And I think every girl\boy in their life, atleast once had felt and can relate Thinovika as I got attached and felt the same as her.

About the Author

Behind the name [Divyasreemagesh] is a dreamer who believes in the power of stories to mend broken hearts. When she isn't writing, she is often found immersed in filmmaking or dancing—two arts that, like words, help her express what cannot be said aloud. She writes to heal, and hopes her readers feel a little less alone within her pages.

Follow her on:
Instagram: [@divyasree_magesh]
youtube: [MD_flimi]

www.ingramcontent.com/pod-product-compliance
Lightning Source LLC
Chambersburg PA
CBHW050015170726
48282CB00025B/408
* 9 7 8 9 3 3 4 4 0 7 1 7 4 *